THE FIRST DAUGHTER

LJ Byrne

Amazon

The characters and events portrayed in this book are fictitious. Any similarity to real persons, living or dead, is coincidental and not intended by the author.

ISBN-13: 9798371023766

Cover design by: Canva.com
Library of Congress Control Number: 2018675309
Printed in the United States of America

To BTS ARMY everywhere, may our 7 always shine a light for us.

To BTS: Kim Namjoon, Kim Seokjin, Min Yoongi, Jung Hoseok, Park Jimin, Kim Taehyung, Jeon Jungkook.

THE FIRST DAUGHTER

I: SECOND NO LONGER

I walk into the courtyard and smile at the excited twitter of voices. "She's here," I hear one young voice say.

Alanna would never sit on the ground the way I do. She would be afraid of the dirt and ruining her clothes, but I don't care as the children clamor around me. Rather than sit on the proffered bench, I join them on the cobbled ground. "Are you here to read to us, princess?" one little girl asks.

"Yes, I am." I smile as my nursemaid, Cymoni, listens by the fountain. She has raised me since birth, taking me from my dead mother's arms. I am too old to have a nurse, but she remains by my side, a cross between a governess and a maid and a friend. Her gray hair is the only hint of her age. Otherwise, her face remains the same – at least to my biased eyes.

To my right, my personal guard Torin. Assigned to me by my father, he is never far from my side. He is both young and old to my eyes. Young in that his energy is unfailing. Old in that he is older than my brother.

"Gather around so I can read," I urge the children. At eighteen, I am still prone to impulsive moments, but they have become less and less. Cymoni says it is because I am growing into womanhood, laughing when I roll my eyes. As the second daughter and third child, to King Roland, I am allowed to read to the children and wander into the city. Unlike my sister, I've been allowed to ride my horse with a great deal of freedom. I've spent nights in the castle libraries, reading tomes on philosophy, math, and history. I've gotten muddy on more than one occasion.

Alanna never approved. "You're like a boy," she often said to me in despair. "So coarse. So rowdy. Unrefined."

As I begin to read, I remind myself that soon Alanna will be a queen. *She will be a married woman tomorrow*, I think to myself. She will make a beautiful queen. I couldn't say much about whether she would be wise or useful, but she would be undoubtedly beautiful.

I finish the brief history of our kingdom – children don't want to hear long, boring stuff. We are small and proud, with a solid army and well-managed borders. "But now, I will tell you about the importance of the First Daughter, in honor of my sister." When the kids giggle, I smile broadly. "The land could only create female things for the land itself."

"It was probably less noisy without boys," says one of the older girls. She is shushed by a teacher, but I single the child out.

"It might have been. Though I know I argued with my sister quite a bit. So perhaps it was very noisy." The child laughs with me. "The first man came, gifted by the heavens, and he was no ordinary man. He had power. He took a wife and had three daughters. The First was wise and fair. The Second was clever. But the Third was jealous. When his wife died, he was so sad that he left, leaving the world to his three daughters. Each daughter was given a piece of land, and with the magic they inherited from their father, they created more people and more animals."

"Why was the Third so jealous?" a boy asks. "She got an equal share."

It is a good question. "I don't know," I answer honestly. "But this is a story, and sometimes stories are exaggerated to make them more entertaining." I can tell the teacher doesn't like my interpretation, but it pays to be royalty. She's not about to scold me in front of others. "The lands prospered, but the lands under the First and Second Daughters prospered even more. The Third was certain her father had given her the worst lands. So, she plotted. She invited her sisters to a great feast, and when they came, she poisoned them." The children gasp even though they've heard this tale before. "But the First didn't sicken right away. When she saw what was happening, she cried out to her father in the skies, and he blessed her one last time. Before she died, she cast her terrible sister to the north, past the mountains, and cursed her to never return. The land absorbed the First and Second and healed itself."

"And since then, the wicked people in the north have never crossed into our lands," the teacher concludes, ignoring my frown.

I have never liked that ending because I could never understand how an entire people could be wicked. There are enough bad people here to leave me to believe that bad sorts are random at best.

I get the bag from Cymoni and deliver the baked goods I'd taken from the palace kitchen. Torin hands the purse full of coin to the lead teacher with careful instructions on how the money is to be used. But as the children mill around me to select a treat, I notice Torin being pulled away by a palace messenger. The man whispers urgently into Torin's ear, and Torin's face grows grave and sad. His eyes flicker towards me.

Cymoni, alert as ever, comes close to my side and gently guides me away from the children.

"What is it?" I ask as Torin approaches. I'm confused when he goes down to one knee. The action is far too solemn.

"Your Highness," he begins, and now I know something terrible has happened, "your sister is dead. The marriage to the Kingdom of Tyre has not happened. Your father wishes you to know that you are now the First Daughter."

II: ARRANGEMENTS

They say work eases grief. I suppose it must be true because I have not been given time to grieve. Given only two weeks to prepare, I must pack and ready myself to become a queen. It is unexpected.

Alanna dreamed of parties and fancy gowns. I dream of books and knowledge. She was a lady – elegant and slim. I am... me. Not always elegant. Cymoni describes me as "solid", and I've taken that to mean that I am not slim. I am tall for a girl, and Father says I have a good disposition. I am not meant to be a queen. I am the spare, the one who is to sit by my father in his old age while my sister bears children far away and my brother rules at home.

As Cymoni helps me dress, I can't remember how my sister last looked when I saw her. Pretty. Alanna was always pretty. Was she nervous? Scared? Eager? I think eager. That would have been Alanna – anxious to make a good impression, eager to dazzle the world. I try not to think of other questions. Did she suffer? Was she aware of her death? Torin tells me I mustn't think of it, or I will go mad.

Before the formalities, Torin takes me to a drawing-room where I meet the envoys. Envoys. That is unexpected. The king of Tyre has sent two enjoys. He must be anxious to secure the alliance.

When I enter, Cymoni and Torin my quiet shadows, I see two men. My brother speaks to them in measured tones. They are young, and there is a faint resemblance in their eyes and the shape of their forehead.

One has dark hair like me and large eyes bright with curiosity and intelligence. There is energy in his body as he makes a point. His physique indicates that he is past his boyish teen years and likely in his early twenties. (Torin has taught me the basics of hand-to-hand combat, and part of the training included estimating your opponent's age based on body size and shape.) Although his demeanor is cheerful, he is dressed in black: black leather, black silk, black shoes. Perhaps he mourns my sister.

The other carries a more aristocratic air with a chiseled jaw and deeper skin. His brown hair has a faint wave to it, and his nose is more sharply defined. He seems older, but not by much. There is an added maturity to the contour of his face whereas the other still has the curve of youth in his cheek. He is serious, only faintly smiling at something.

My brother Ronan extends his hand when he sees me. My gown is dark blue velvet – dark enough for mourning but not too depressing since I'm about to be married by proxy. This is my fate today – cement the alliance between Tyre and Fernwald. One of these men will stand in for the king.

I am my brother's favorite, and we are alike in many ways. Although he is more physical than I am, we love long walks, books, and history. We are curious about science and wonder about how the victors have rewritten history. When our hands meet, the involuntary clench tells me more than words. He will miss me. I will miss him. And that will hurt as much, if not more, as the loss of a sister who we loved because she was kin.

"Gentlemen, my sister, Illyria." When my brother introduces me, I manage a curtsey, but I don't demurely lower my head, pretending to be shy. Instead, I watch both men for their reactions.

The younger one is curious. The other hides his surprise. No doubt, they have compared me to my sister's beauty and find me wanting. "Two envoys?" I ask the question pointedly. "And which one of you will be the king's proxy?"

The younger one speaks first, inclining his sable head. "Princess, I am Kol. My brother Kel is the king."

Something in Kei's words makes the other one angry. "We are both brothers to the king," he corrects Kei with a glare. "I am Kei."

I'd studied enough of Tyre's history to know they were fond of monosyllabic names – something to do with making it easier to shout on the battlefield. This means that I know about the controversy surrounding the king and his two brothers.

In Tyre, the king is permitted a wife and a royal concubine. The children born from either woman are legitimate, although the wife's children take precedence. Kol is the son of the royal concubine. His mother was a slave, but his father saw her, fell in love, and made her his concubine. Kei, on the other hand, was born of an affair between the king and one of his wife's ladies; technically, he is illegitimate and cannot inherit the throne.

Here's the issue. Kei's mother is from a powerful house within Tyre. A widow when she tangled with the king, there were rumors the king intended to make her his concubine... Until he saw Kol's mother. With Kol's mother's low birth, many within Tyre believe the king's immediate heir should be Kei, not Kol.

"Neither trusted the other so you both came," I surmise. Both men look at me in surprise, but my brother hides a smile. He knows I am prone to being direct. The dress feels stuffy, and I am anxious to be done with the day. "Very well, Prince Kol. Shall we formalize this?"

Kei processes my words for a full five seconds before he blinks. His face shifts subtly, and instead of the curious young man, there is a hint of primal authority in his demeanor. I find the change curious.

His brother watches as Kol takes my hand from Ronan's and guides me to the antechamber where we will formalize the vows to cement me to Tyre.

III: NOT FAR NOW

"Are you sure you wouldn't prefer the carriage?" Kei asks me for the third time.

Torin coughs. We are on our third day of travel, and I have been in the carriage from time to time, but I find it stifling and boring. I fix my hat and slide a glance at Kei. Kol is silent. Kol is to my right, Torin to my left, and Kei is to Torin's left. "Have I been complaining?" I ask pointedly.

Kei flushes when Kol snorts. They exchange the usual glare. "You are different from your sister," Kol says suddenly.

The change in topic is awkward. Torin shifts. We are both wary, and rightly so. If a throne is at stake, who would benefit from a king losing his betrothed? And how will this person – or persons – react when I arrive, married in name already to the king? This is why Kol and Kei are here. They suspect each other, and that is far from irrational. Each has the potential to gain if the king produces no heir.

"We are two sides of the same coin," I say, marking their reactions. Kol is taken aback, but Kei narrows his eyes at me.

In the past three days, to keep me from thinking of Ronan and Alanna, I have studied these two men. Kol is more introspective of the two. Kei more vocal. Both have had the benefit of a strong education and physical training thanks to the benefits of their birth. Despite Kei's questionable legitimacy, his father insisted Kei live in the palace among his brothers. It no doubt led to more infighting than harmony among political factions.

As the guards create a makeshift campsite so the horses can rest for an hour, the princes come to my side. I decline both their offered hands and dismount on my own. Cymoni and Torin have created a canopied area near some trees to provide shade, but the princes react with various levels of consternation when I move a box or two to use as seats. "I have two hands like most people," I state, not caring if they deem me unfeminine. I have never liked to be waited on, and I have no intention of changing to please them. Cymoni gets water for me while Torin leaves to confer with the guards. He knows my old nurse can defend me easily. I have seen her in action.

Awkward silence lasts but a few minutes. "Were you close with your sister?" Kol asks. Kei flashes him an annoyed frown.

I hesitate. "We were and were not alike, Alanna and I," I begin, wandering into memories of my childhood. "As children, she mothered me, and I want to believe we were close then. But she was First Daughter, destined to some prestigious marriage. She tired of games and preferred dresses over books." Tears threaten my composure, but I will them back. Not yet. Not now. There will be time to properly grieve for Alanna. I remind myself that I am doing this out of duty to my family. A substitute First Daughter.

"Siblings do change when duty calls," Kei responds in a flat tone. "People change, princess, when crowns and wealth are at stake."

Kol's lips flatten into a thin line, and he is annoyed with Kei's behavior. He averts his head for a moment. "You were saying, princess, that you preferred books over dresses. You were the studious child."

"My brother and I..." I trail off. I could imagine Ronan whispering, *Be strong. We are together under the vast sky.* "We were into books. History. Alanna was not so keen on her studies. I suppose the last strong memory I have of her was her twelfth birthday. It was a turning point. She would be schooled in graces and art, and I was to be left to my own devices. I bought a wooden jewelry box and lined it with velvet. In my mind, I thought I was an artist. I painted flowers on the box. Childish, silly flowers in blue and yellow. When I presented it to her, she smiled and told me she would treasure it always." My voice wobbles, but I steady myself with a deep breath. "At the time, I only marked at how formally she spoke to me. I thought she was putting a distance between us with her words. But now, a tad wiser, I can see her kindness. She could've laughed at my scribbles." The two princes listen to me keenly, both affected in different ways. I feel compelled to ask. "Did you see her before—" I break off. "Was she happy?"

Kol lowers his eyes, focusing on the ground before him. I wonder how he isn't sweating to death in his dark clothes. I'm warm in my lighter riding gown and hat, and I'm grateful for the breeze. "I don't think she suffered. The poison was quick. She and her guard…" He doesn't finish, and I am glad.

Alanna is buried in Tyre. It is not my wish nor Ronan's – I would see her next to our mother – but King Kel means to be kind by including her in the royal tombs. "I am glad to hear," I breathe. It was quick. I am glad it was quick. "And yet, no one knows who poisoned her?"

"We questioned the staff," Kei informs me

I need to change the subject. "What is there to know about my – husband?" The word is awkward on my tongue. I am not ready to be a wife. I am nineteen and prone to flights of fancy. I am a scholar, an observer. I am not wife material. Too stubborn and opinionated, I am not one to defer to another's wishes.

"Kel is kind," Kol says, and there is love in his voice. "Sometimes too kind. He likes to be happy." A hint of doubt. "He is skilled in archery. He dances well. Women find him attractive."

"Is he learned? Does he like books?"

Kei leans forward to look at me curiously. "Books? Did you say books?" Mirth dances in his eyes.

"Yes, books. That thing with pages bound together filled with words and sometimes pictures." I can't help the saucy reply. Cymoni, silently putting things into order behind Kei, hides her twitching lips. Kei blinks, thinking and assessing. I wonder what he's concluded.

Kol ventures to respond. "He has a great library that is

popular with scholars. You wish to study our books?"

It's hard to temper my enthusiasm. "I do. I love to learn. I am anxious to read your history books and compare them to ours."

"You will find, princess, that our brother is not much of a scholar." This from Kei. And then, with a wry smile, "You will find all of us lacking in that department."

Kol's guileless eyes shine in the sun. Will Kel favor Kol's looks or Kei's? "You think our history books will be different?" Kol asks out loud.

"Haven't you wondered?" I gesture at the horizon. "All this land controlled by three women. The myth of the First Daughter. Fernwald continues to uphold tradition, but Tyre does not."

"What use is there when no First Daughter has had any powers to speak of?" Kei challenges me. "Yes, our history books say for a while the royal bloodlines may have had powers, but for years the First Daughters have been nothing more than pretty ornaments. Why do we stick to foolish traditions rather than progressing? At least, in Tyre, we stopped revering First Daughters. My brother tried to marry a First and gets a Second, and no one really cares."

Torin has rejoined us, and his hand rests on the pommel of his sword. A word and he will draw his sword out of loyalty to me; he owes none to Fernwald nor Tyre. But I am not that kind of person. I hold Kei's gaze until he backs down.

"Brother, she is Kel's wife and will be crowned queen. She will be *your* queen," Kol says in a hard voice, and his grave expression changes the angles of his face. He is somehow older, and he exudes a level of authority I haven't seen before. "You should mind your words."

"It doesn't bother me," I say impulsively. "I prefer blunt words. I value honesty."

Kei's laugh strikes me as bitter. "Then you're going to a bad place for that. Tell me, *sister*, what do you think of our fascination with *royal concubines*?

The notion of a royal concubine makes me feel uneasy. It hadn't bothered Alanna. In fact, she'd hoped it meant her husband wouldn't visit her as often. But in Fernwald, there was a king and his queen and no one else. There were no second wives or concubines or harems. I don't know my husband, but I would hope to like him. Can I knowing that he could take a concubine at any moment? Yes, my children would be above any with a concubine, but why muddle the waters already riddled with castes and titles?

My sister was a great beauty. I am plain. I don't expect the king to see me with desire, but I hope for friendship. Anything to make the marriage tolerable. But what if King Kel doesn't feel the same way? A royal concubine is often selected for love. He will love her. I suppose he will try to tolerate me.

"Kei, you go too far! Our brother will hear of this," Kol snaps.

Kei doesn't hide his annoyance or anger. "I have a right to be curious about what our future queen thinks of concubines. To think Kel chose you to be his proxy." Disdain colors his face. "Your mother was nothing, Kol. A slave. She didn't even know how to write. You are younger than me, yet you dare to correct me?"

Cymoni has turned to watch, and she exchanges a glance with Torin who rests a hand on his sword. *Watch and learn*, Ronan would say to me when we came across people squabbling. Kei's words have found their mark. Kol is struck silent, and there is triumph in Kei's face. But then Kol looks up and says, "I am the son of a slave. And you are the son of..." He doesn't finish his words, but Kei grows pale with rage.

"I suppose the concept of concubines was to ensure a male heir," I say carefully. "But it is not my place to change what is accepted in Tyre." My brow furrows a little as I consider how horrible the concept of slavery is. I sigh. "Of course, what do I know? As you said, Prince Kei, I am a false First Daughter your brother is marrying." Kei's mouth snaps shut.

I am about to suggest we restart our journey when the attack happens.

IV: FIGHT

The arrow comes out of nowhere – at least, to my unpracticed eye – and strikes a soldier in the front. Do I imagine the thud when the arrow strikes, or do I hear it? I don't know. He falls with a wordless cry, and all I can think is that he wasn't the intended target.

Bandits? Or something more nefarious? Briefly, I think of my sister and wonder. When the men appear, I take in their weapons, attire, and gear. No, not random. These men are well-armed and well-equipped. Someone knew we would be here on this particular road.

"Get into the carriage, now!" Torin barks as Cymoni drags me towards the carriage. Both princes have pulled their swords, Kei calling for shields while Kol mounts his horse and circles our camp. I learned strategy alongside my brother – I was bored, and no one paid much attention to my shenanigans – so I'm aware of what Kol is doing. He is looking for an exit strategy. Not for him but for me. Our eyes meet as Cymoni tries to toss me into the carriage, but I resist as much as possible.

"If we fall, grab the princess and race to the port!" Kol shouts at Torin, gesturing to the west. "There are more than enough men there to protect her! We will hold them off!"

They can't do that! Kol and Kei are the king's brothers, his current heirs until he has a son. But Kol turns because the armed men are closer, and he doesn't hesitate to charge into the fray. When the two sides clash, I note three archers remaining at a distance. They could've killed more of our men before engaging, so why did they hold back?

Despite being tiny and older, Cymoni strong-arms me into the carriage; this time, I go willingly. There is storage beneath the seats, and I am specifically looking for one box. "No, child, you need to stay in here," Cymoni says to me, thin fingers on my arm, eyes severe. "Let the men fight."

"I can help," I insist. "Cymoni!"

Gray eyes meet mine – gray like her hair, gray like her history. "If I say run, will you run?"

"Yes, but the other side is not shooting." When her eyes grow wide as she understands my meaning, I say, "Exactly. So let me do something here."

My brother's gift to me: a beautiful bow with arrows. My wedding gift. I pull out the bow, customized for me with the strong, but flexible wood our kingdom is famed for. Then I grab the arrows and rush back out.

I have never killed a man, and I don't intend to start today. While my sister learned to dance, I learned battlefield tactics. While my sister sang and learned music, I read philosophy. And while she learned how to stitch pretty flowers on silk, I learned how to use a bow. I aim, well-aware of the force my bow would deliver.

My first arrow hits the first archer in the thigh. His scream confuses the attackers and gives our soldiers an advantage. The second archer notices me too late as the arrow catches him in the shoulder. Kei, blocking a hit, sees me, his mouth open as I aim again. The distraction costs him, and he takes a blow to his side. Luckily for him, the blow is not a sword, and his leathers hold, but the grimace of pain tells me he is in danger. The soldier protecting him falls, and I change targets. Before Kei's attacker strikes with a sword, my arrow cuts the skin at his throat. It isn't immediately fatal, but that no longer matters. Kei sees his opening and drives a dagger through the man's skull.

Kol is at the front of the fight, and his sword moves efficiently and unerringly. The sword rises, and the flash of metal dims with blood. Torin guards his back, and the two bring death to the enemy. Torin doesn't hesitate to dispatch the injured archers, but it's Kol who chases the third one down. A spray of blood follows his strike.

For a minute, I stare at the injured and the dead. We have only lost two. But the fifteen men who came at us are dead. Torin and Kol rush to me on horses.

"Are you hurt?" Torin. To the point.

But Kol is angry. "What do you think you're doing? Why would you put yourself at risk?" He has a bruise on his cheek but is otherwise unarmed.

Kei holds a hand to his ribs as he joins his half-brother. They assess each other for injuries before feigning indifference. "Are you insane?" he gasps at me.

"Perhaps I am, but I am not going to leave you here to die," I snap. Some of the adrenaline has faded and sweat trickles down my neck.

"She saved your life," Torin grunts at Kei. "I have taught her since she was a child. She knows what she is doing."

"You put yourself at risk!" Kol shouts, and his beautiful face darkens. "We had it under control."

I say nothing, pinning him with my eyes until his words dry up. Then, and only then, I say, "We must burn the bodies and bury our men. And then we need to get to the port immediately. The archers could have cut us down, Kol, but they only fired once."

Kol's expression is stony, but the flicker in his eyes tells me he understands. The archers didn't fire because they didn't want to kill their intended target: me.

V: NO ORDINARY PRINCESS

Our entourage hobbles into the port where a ship waits for us. Kol did not lie when he said there would be soldiers here aplenty. We arrive smaller than expected, injured, footsore. We take off immediately, crossing the bay to reach Tyre.

This is not how I wanted to arrive in Tyre: tired, dirty, agitated. I won't arrive the way Alanna did: calm, elegant, beautiful. I'm rushed to the castle under heavy guard, Kol by my elbow. It isn't until I'm placed in temporary apartments that I get a moment to breathe.

Alone with Cymoni and Torin, I try and assess what is happening. Torin checks the apartment for possible hidden rooms where someone might be spying. Once he deems it relatively secure, he asks, "You know the attackers were coming for you, don't you? I don't like this one bit."

I nod. "The archers held off. We could've easily been swarmed, but their actions allowed me to pick them off one by one." My wedding ring – a large ruby embedded in gold – is heavy on my finger.

Cymoni goes through my wardrobe, trying to find something suitable for me to wear. "They have spring-fed baths here," she says, "so you'll have time to clean up before you meet the king. And I agree that the attackers miscalculated. The big question is whether we think one of the princes was involved."

My brows come together. "What do you mean? They both defended me."

Cymoni's sharp eyes flicker. "So they did. But who else knew we would be on that road? And who stands to gain if the king fails to take a queen."

Torin scratches his beard. "Everything must be checked before she eats," he tells Cymoni. "I will inspect the security myself. Do not greet the king without me."

When he leaves, Cymoni helps me out of my travel-stained dress. The spring-fed bath is delightfully warm. I quickly wash my hair and scrub my skin clean, doing my best to get the grime out from my nails. Once I'm clean, Cymoni braids my damp hair – it won't dry fast enough so this is the best we can do to avoid looking completely wild – and helps me into my dress. Alanna was the tall, slender one. While I am not fat, I do have a solid build. No one describes me as willowy or thin. I have never been vain, but standing in front of the mirror, I wonder if the king will be disappointed at the plain Second Daughter. No, I remind myself, I am First Daughter now. My hands clench.

"Come, come," Cymoni scolds me, "you must smile and be pleasant. A man will prefer a pleasant wife over anything else."

There's a gentle knock on the door, and then a lovely woman enters. She isn't very tall, but her curvaceous figure is alluring and well-proportioned. Even her walk is sensual. Her smile is open and friendly. "Your Highness, welcome to Tyre," she says in a low, melodious voice. "I am Lady Tassia of Caldor. I've come to see if there is anything you need."

I return her smile. She seems sweet and engaging. "No, I think I have everything I need."

She shakes her pretty head in dismay. "I heard about what happened on the road. How appalling." Tilting her head, she scans me. "But you were so brave. Why, Prince Kol has told the king how you picked off the enemy. You will be a warrior queen, no doubt."

Cymoni, going through my shoes, glances at Lady Tassia, but I haven't a clue what she's thinking. Her face is devoid of expression.

Lady Tassia admires my dress. "What fine linen! We prefer silks here, but that is a beautiful dress." She brushes a fair hand against the pale silk gown she's wearing. "It must be very hard to come here and take your sister's place." She grabs my hand. "I hope you will love Tyre as much as I do. And I hope we become very good friends."

"I would like that very much."

A maid comes in carrying wood for the fireplace. Lady Tassia leans over and whispers, "Be careful. This is your maid, but she was your sister's once. She gave the princess much grief and ruined many things." Straightening, she says loudly, "Cosra, make sure the princess has enough wood for the night and clean the fireplace before you leave the wood."

The maid, a girl no older than me, glowers at Lady Tassia. She drops the bucket noisily. "Yes, my lady," she bites out. Pale eyes flicker over me dismissively before she storms out.

Tassia sighs. "I'm afraid you'll have to make do. But once you're Queen, you can change the household as you see fit. I will see you at dinner tonight. The king is hosting it in your honor, of course." Her eyes twinkle. "King Kel is very handsome. I think you'll like him immensely."

"She seems nice," I say to Cymoni after Lady Tassia leaves. "I hope we do become friends."

Cymoni is silent. She pulls out blue silk slippers. "This will complement the blue in your dress," she says, reaching over to smooth a fold. Her sharp eyes look over my shoulder. "I see the prince is here to escort you."

Prince Kol enters dressed in deep red and black. It's been so hectic that I haven't had a chance to organize my thoughts on him. The dramatic colors suit him, offsetting his lightly golden skin. He cuts a striking figure with his broad shoulders and toned body. I remember how easily he held the sword when he fought. "Your Highness." He bows, formal and polite. "I am here to present you to the king, my brother."

Torin is behind the prince, so when Kol extends his hand to me, I take it, mindful that I need Torin close to me while I figure out who to trust. From a distance, Kol and I appear as a young couple taking a measured walk. I am conscious that my dress is conservative with its high-neck and simple cut. My attire has always been more about function rather than fashion, and there wasn't enough time to create new gowns before I left. With my damp braid, I wonder how drab I look in comparison to Tyre's colorful court.

"Kel is holding a smaller audience out of consideration to you," Kol tells me as we reach one of the side halls. "Only key courtiers will be here." Pause. "Kei is already there. I will take you in and present you to the king. You will curtsey. He will come and offer his hand." He's quickly running down the order of events, perhaps sensing my nervousness.

"Alright." My heart thumps loudly in my chest, and I begin to worry about how clammy my hands are.

The doors open, and Kol guides me with elegant steps. Do princes here get trained how to walk? My brother was taught to walk with a stiff back, but Kol saunters in like he owns the carpet. As I walk towards the man who is legally my husband, I focus on him. I now know that good lucks must be a family trait. The king has Kol's lower full lip, but where Kol's upper lip is thinner with a well-defined bow, King Kel's mouth is a complete pout. His nose is finer than Kol's, which is more button-shaped and larger, but not as defined and aristocratic as Kei's. Whereas Kei has a square-shaped face and Kol has a more circular one, the king's face is oval, symmetrical, with a soft jawline. His brown hair brushes his shoulder, and a charming lock drapes a cheek. He is breathlessly handsome.

I lower my eyes first, hoping that my action seems demure rather than flustered. When we reach the foot of the dais, Kol allows me to sink into a deep curtsey. I wobble only a little.

"Your Majesty, may I introduce Princess Ilyria of Fernwald?" Kol announces me in a firm, deep voice.

Alanna was the graceful one. I was taught the basics. I hear the rustle of fine cloth, and I know the king approaches my crouched person. A fine, elegant hand is extended. "Welcome, princess, to my court." As I take the hand and rise, the king turns to his assembled court. "I have taken Princess Ilyria as my wife. Our wedding took place by proxy. Tomorrow my bride will be crowned and become Queen of Tyre."

An excited twitter passes through the hall, and I finally look at my husband, searching for any signs of disappointment. He only gives me a kind smile before patting my hand. I climb the dais with him and am seated on a small chair to his left. I'm surprised to see Lady Tassia standing behind the king's chair. My puzzlement grows when he takes her hand and kisses it passionately.

People begin to talk as the king tells me that he must attend to the merchants coming before we can talk privately. "I'm told you've met Lady Tassia. As my Royal Concubine, she's been controlling the ladies of the court, but you will run things once you are crowned queen."

Royal Concubine. When I stare at Tassia, her smile is cold and triumphant, and I come to a sinking realization. Her actions earlier were to disarm me so that the pain and humiliation of this moment would be ingrained in my memory. I look at Kol, and from the way he evades my eyes, and the way Kei is expressionless, I know. They deliberately did not mention her to me. Now the questions by Kei before the attack make sense.

I can hear my brother warning me to think before I act. *Remember, Ily, when the tables turn on you, stop. Don't react. You have a better chance of winning if they think the first strike has missed.*

I learned statecraft by Ronan's side, but I never played court games. I suppose it's time for me to learn.

VI: RIGHT OF MOURNING

I can't bring myself to look at Torin or Cymoni from my chair. Normally they are by my side, but right now, they are far away. *When I am queen,* I begin in my head and then stop. For now, I am isolated while the king tends to daily matters. My heart thuds painfully in my chest as I wonder how many of the courtiers know that I came here ignorant. I am incapable of reacting and unwilling to look at anyone, but I manage to keep my stony expression. Ronan would be proud.

Once court is dismissed, I'm led to a small receiving chamber. Torin joins me with a grave face, and I am glad Lady Tassia is absent. Kol and Kei join their brother. They avoid my direct look. Do they feel a shred of shame?

"I'm glad you made it here safely," the king says, accepting a glass of wine from Kol. "My brothers were anxious for your safety."

"Thank you. They were – kind and considerate on our trip." If King Kel notes the sarcasm, he doesn't react. Inwardly, I want to throw a tantrum, but I maintain a façade of calm.

Kel exchanges a glance with his brothers before turning to me. Again, I look to see if he is disappointed by the girl he sees. I can't say. "It is tradition for a crowned queen to request a favor of the king and for the king to grant it," Kel says with a slight smile. "As long as it is within my power to grant." He leans towards me. "I believe your sister wanted to have the royal jewels redone."

When he mentions my sister, I gather my nerve. "I request the Right of Mourning," I say in a steady voice. "My only sister is dead, and I would like time to mourn her properly."

Silence, but I think I see relief flicker over the king's face. In comparison to Tassia, I am dull and colorless, so perhaps he is glad he doesn't have to bed me tonight. Invoking the Right of Mourning is a risk. I am here to be a queen and mother to heirs, not to mourn a sister even though she was murdered. But I don't care. When I become the Queen, my heirs will take precedence over the Royal Concubine, so it doesn't matter if she gives birth to an heir before I do.

The truth is that I'm not ready for the marriage bed. And now that whatever game Lady Tassia has begun, I need to reevaluate the board and the players before I act. My life might depend on it. There is no shame in asking. This much I know. I lift my chin to tell the king that he may be king, but I will be treated fairly.

King Kel nods his head with regal ease. "Of course," he says in a soothing way. "Brothers, witness that I will honor my wife's request. I understand this marriage was unexpected and sudden, but an alliance with Fernwald is important. Or so my advisors say."

I don't find his humor particularly funny, but I decide to laugh anyway. Kol starts and recovers.

My reaction pleases the king. "I understand, Princess Ilyria, that you are learned. May I call you Ilyria?"

I incline my head.

"Ilyria. There are many things I must do as king, and I hope that when you are my queen, you will share those burdens with me."

"Of course." Again, I hear Ronan's voice advising me. *Play nice even if you don't feel like it, little sister. Never move to strike in an obvious way.*

"I intend to retain Sir Torin as my personal guard," I say. "And Lady Cymoni will continue to attend me."

The king salutes me with a cup. "That is your right and prerogative. I can see you are well versed in much. I wish we had more time to talk, but I have promised Tassia a ride today, so I cannot stay long and linger."

Interesting. I am complimented and dismissed in a breath.

When does a king have so much time for idle activities?

"It is proper before being crowned to rest and reflect," my husband continues. "Therefore, I will see you in the morning." He parts the curtain and waves at some guards to walk him to the stables.

Torin eyes me expectantly, but I don't intend to leave just yet. "Gentlemen," I begin, and the two princes have the grace to look ashamed. The pain lingers in my chest. I consider my next words carefully. "I am wed to your brother, the King of Tyre. Tomorrow I officially become your queen." I indicate that Torin should escort me from the receiving chamber. "I value honesty and truth. I hope you both pay attention to that."

VII: QUEEN

The gown delivered to my room is heavy and ornate. The pearl buttons number in the hundreds and it takes Cymoni and Cosra forever to do them all. Velvet adds to the weight and does not flatter me. I can't wait for the coronation to be over. The deep red color is unflattering against my skin. My only change is a silk sash tied to my right arm: a symbol of mourning.

When I look in the mirror, I can't help but think that I look like a rolled-up carpet. Alanna had a lithe, womanly figure. She would have carried the dress with regal glamour. I am shapeless. I think Cosra smirks. Perhaps Lady Tassia didn't lie completely.

"Come, come," Cymoni snaps, brushing Cosra aside. "I will finish this up. You, girl, go on with your duties."

Cosra's face goes rigid, but then she lowers her eyes. "Excuse me, Your Highness." She barely dips as she takes her leave.

"That one would poison your drink in an instant, I think," Cymoni says, ever blunt. "Are you angry with those pathetic princes, my love?"

I continue to glower at my reflection. "No, I am not angry," I answer honestly. Hurt? Yes. Disappointed? Yes. I pick up the book I read last night. "This was helpful, Cymoni. I know what I will ask for."

Cymoni knows me well, and I am grateful that she and Torin stay by my side. I would be lonely otherwise. "I can't wait to hear it. Be sure to hold your head up. You are to be a queen."

Feeling like a sausage, I stiffly walk out where Torin waits with a handful of guards from Tyre. If he thinks I look ridiculous, he doesn't say, only indicating which way I should walk. I feel like

I'm carrying a weight of rocks with this gown. Cymoni follows behind me until we reach the great hall.

My hands tremble as I wait for the doors to open, and I quickly hide them in the long sleeves. As the door opens, the first person I see is Lady Tassia. She is in a bright red silk gown with gold trim, and her gown glitters in the light. When she sees me, her obvious smile is meant to make me feel self-conscious. I feel my cheeks burn, but I remember Cymoni's words and hold my head high. I wait until she bows deep. For all that I despise castes and social hierarchy, I intend for her to remember that I am now Queen. Then I step onto the carpet leading towards the dais.

There, at the bottom of the dais, King Kel waits with a man in gray robes. I see the pillow with the consort's crown. As I pass by the court, the women curtsey, and the men fall to one knee. Behind me, I know Lady Tassia follows at a distance. I feel a touch of pity for her. Perhaps the king loves her, but she has no power, no voice, because she is merely a potential source of heirs to the King's Council.

A pillow is provided for me to kneel as the man in gray asks me questions. Will I uphold the laws of Tyre? Will I fulfill my duty and obligation as Tyre's queen? I say the correct responses.

The crown is heavy, and the edge cuts into my skin as a reminder that I can't take this responsibility lightly. I'm glad a queen is only required to wear this crown for important ceremonies, or I would be constantly afflicted with headaches. It's Kel's hand that helps me to my feet – and mercifully, I don't stumble under the weight of my clothes. He kisses me on both cheeks – his lips are soft, squishy, and a little moist – before placing a medallion around my neck.

The royal family in Tyre has not produced daughters for a number of years, and the medallion is one the Tyre royal family has granted to the First Daughters when it had them. My fingers touch the medallion, and a sense of familiarity flows through me. The onyx jewel at the center is the size of a grape and is strangely warm. I must be imagining things.

He takes my cold and clammy hand and leads me up the

steps to our thrones – the queen's chair is a handspan lower than the king's – and we turn to face the applauding court. King Kel holds his hand up for silence. To his left, Kol and Kei watch stoically.

"I present to you Queen Ilyria… of Tyre!" the king says loudly, and bright cheers flood the hall. I maintain my rigid smile, noting Tassia sneaking to the corner to be close to the king. "Following tradition, I grant my new bride and queen one favor in her honor." He looks at me expectantly.

"Your Majesty, my lords and ladies," I say in a low voice, so I don't sound childish. "I have studied your laws and the laws of the land. My request is this: let there be no more slaves in Tyre." When a rumble of surprise begins to ripple through, I quickly add, "Fernwald has long prospered without slavery. I have studied your lands and economies, and Tyre is capable of the same. It is the king's prerogative that determines whether slavery is allowed." I disengage my hand and sink as gracefully as I can to the floor – it is likely I look like I've fallen on my tush – and say, "Your Majesty, if you grant this, I will assist you in this endeavor and work with you to ease the transition among your lords."

I've shocked the court and the king – my face continues to nearly kiss the floor. "Gracious lady," the king begins in his cultured, smooth voice as he helps me rise. His brown eyes search mine curiously. "I grant your favor."

The court bursts into noisy chatter, and I finally take a close look at those around me. There is some resentment, but more than a few eyes me with cautious interest. To be honest, I hadn't expected the king to acquiesce right away, but now that he has, I want his court to see that while I may be a substitute bride, I intend to be a proper queen. Kei is pale and subdued, and again he seems to be assessing and evaluating me. Of greater interest is Kol. The younger prince's wide eyes – so easily deemed sincere and guileless – are equal parts confused and ashamed. More than a few lords look at him and wonder.

I have not forgotten that Kol's mother was a slave before she became the Royal Concubine. I have more than a few questions regarding that. But my interest in ending slavery has nothing to do with Kol and has everything to do with social justice.

After the initial noise fades, the king dismisses the court and heads to the Council's chambers with me and Torin in tow. We stop at the doors.

"My dear," he says, holding my hands in his. His handsome face is even more devastating up close, and my heart hammers a little louder. "I am afraid I've developed a headache. And I promised Tassia a walk in the park. As my queen, you are also my representative. Would you be so kind to oversee the Council and decide on matters in my name? If you have any questions, we can discuss them over dinner."

My mouth hangs open. "You want me to lead your Council?" I ask stupidly.

He has the grace to blush. "It would be a great opportunity for you to discuss the slavery matter," he says, eyes pleading.

"I-I suppose." I face the doors. When I turn back, my husband is gone, and only Torin remains, his impassive face holding back judgment.

The Council's doors open. Inside, Kei and Kol look for their brother, and when they don't find him, they look at me. Neither seem surprised. I am starting to understand what is wrong with this court and kingdom.

There are two state chairs, and with purposeful movements I take the smaller one. "Gentlemen, the king has asked that I represent him today as my first duty as Queen of Tyre. My earlier request has no doubt left some of you with concerns. I suggest we table that for today to give us time to fully address those concerns for the well-being of Tyre. Does anyone have any issues with that?"

A man with a prominent mustache bows to me. "Your Majesty, I am Count Andes and the senior at the Council. I agree with your request."

"Excellent." I scan their faces, holding Kei's and Kol's a second longer than others to gauge their reaction, before I sit. "Then... Shall we begin?"

VIII: ALANNA'S TOMB

I attend more meetings on my husband's behalf than I can understand. I now see the reservations both Kei and Kol had about Kel. My husband is grateful to have a diligent and hard-working wife, and while I don't mind the work, I find it curious that no one is surprised. Has the king always been this indolent?

By the second week, I find my rhythm. Now I am ready to see Alanna. I take only Torin and Cymoni with me, of course. There is no one else to trust.

I descend into the royal crypt with Cymoni, leaving Torin at the entrance to chat with the guards. Cymoni verifies that the crypt only holds dead bodies before she gives me privacy.

Because Alanna was not crowned before she died, and because she exchanged no wedding vows, her tomb is simple. Her name. A sketched picture. There are flowers that may have been placed by the silent men and women who care for the crypt.

My fingers trace my sister's name. "I hope you did not suffer, Alanna. Do not think I have forgotten. I am still trying to understand this court. Did it confuse you too?" Tears begin to fall. "You would laugh, of course, if you saw how very little the king desires me. I am relieved. He is kind enough, I suppose. Frankly, I'm relieved he finds me so useful."

I glance at the other tombs. Some have statues, gracefully solemn. Others have inscriptions or etchings. My sister will disappear into obscurity.

There are voices at the entrance, but I don't turn to see who enters the crypt. Torin and Cymoni would never let me come to harm.

Footsteps, quiet and hesitant, approach me. Out of my peripheral vision, Kol comes into view. I ignore him. I suppose Torin couldn't refuse the prince entry to the crypt.

Kol glances at me, but then he goes to one of the tombs with a relief of a woman, benevolent and smiling. "Your Majesty, this is my mother," he says suddenly.

I hide my annoyance at no longer being alone and remain silent.

"She died when I was six." When I continue to ignore him, he says, "Your sister mentioned your mother died giving birth to you, but I presume you still miss her." He stares at the carved features. "This is not how my mother was. She was sad. Always sad."

Kol's mother had been a slave. Is he here because I intend to outlaw slavery?

"You know my mother was a slave, but what you don't know is that she didn't want to become my father's concubine. She wasn't given a choice because she was sold to the king." He turns to me. "Father wanted her. He was obsessed with her. Do you know how she died?"

I shake my head.

"When I was six, she came to me one night. I didn't understand when she bundled me in a coat and carried me to the stables. I became scared and began to cry. Guards heard us, recognized me. They didn't recognize my mother because she was in commoner clothes. They thought I was being kidnapped. My mother tripped and dropped me." His breathing becomes ragged. "And a guard killed her. She was escaping, you see. She was trying to flee my father."

"That's... terrible."

"I often wonder what would have happened if I hadn't been afraid." The torches cast their golden light on his face, transforming his face into an echo of the young boy he had been: confused, scared, horrified. "Slaves are being freed around Tyre. Already, the common folk love you. The nobility not so much. But I wanted to thank you." He swallows hard. "I know I have no right to ask for forgiveness. What I did was cruel."

I stare at the effigy that is supposed to resemble Kol's mother. The shape of the eyes match. "I had hoped we would become friends," I say.

Kol lowers his head. "Is that not possible?"

"Was it your intention to be malicious regarding Lady Tassia?"

Kol sucks in his breath, the angles of his face accentuated by shadows. "No. To be honest, I thought you would be more like your sister and... That doesn't excuse me. It wasn't right of me or Kei to do what we did, and I am deeply ashamed."

More like my sister? I find his words curious. "I did not make my request of the king because of you. At least, not directly. I asked it because it is what I want to do." I turn towards him. "Once lost, trust must be earned." I hold my hand out, expecting him to shake it. "But I could use a friend. I hope that one day we *can* call each other friends."

Astonishment fades into something else as Kol looks at me with large eyes that remind me of a fawn. Right now, the decisive action he portrayed on the field is nowhere to be seen – there's almost an innocent vulnerability about him. He takes my hand between his – his fingers are not as long as Kel's, but they are graceful and attractive, belying the strength he possesses – and stares at it for a few seconds. Then he presses a kiss to the back.

I remember how Kel's kiss felt very soft and moist. I found it a bit unpleasant. But Kol's touch is different. The feel of his lips on my is both gentle and firm. It is not overly wet, and my heart skips a beat. I am glad for the poor lighting.

I pull my hand free, pretending to straighten my skirt so Kol doesn't notice my discomfiture. "I will see it done. People must have some freedom to choose."

"You are not what we – what I expected." Kol's words remind me of an earlier thought.

"What do you mean?" I press.

Kol releases my hand and clasps his hands behind his back. Once more, his gaze turns towards his mother. "I don't think we got along," he finally says to me in measured tones. "She would never have fought back, I think, when we were attacked."

I don't rise defensively. He is being politely critical, and he isn't wrong. Alanna wouldn't have fought. "We were not as close as we got older," I admit, "and there were times when she was difficult. But she had no freedoms. From the moment she turned twelve, every aspect of her life was controlled because she was the firstborn daughter. And I think... it would have been easy to resent the freedoms I had."

Kol looks at his mother's tomb once more. "Sometimes it isn't easy being the youngest either," he says.

We stand together in agreeable silence.

IX: A COUNSEL OF COUNCILS

"I am having a few dresses made for you," Cymoni says as she braids my hair and coils it up.

"Oh?" I frown. I don't want to be frivolous with money.

"Don't worry," Cymoni soothes me, "but don't get upset. These were dresses Alanna had made for her. We will use the cloth and make a few changes."

I become silent as I think about that. In the corner, Cosra sweeps the fireplace clean of ashes, but no matter how diligent she looks, I suspect she hears everything. "It's important," I say quietly, "that the Council take me seriously."

"You are Queen," Cymoni replies just as softly. "You must look the part, and your old dresses don't fit here. You are no longer Fernwald's daughter." In the mirror, our eyes meet. "You are worried that the lords will not listen to you today."

For all that the king has promised me the end of slavery, we still must have buy in from the lords or risk unrest. Because this is "my request", the king thinks I am best suited to champion it. I am careful not to criticize the king publicly or privately, but it is painfully obvious the king has little interest in conflict. Or ruling, for that matter.

"I'll tell Torin you are ready," Cymoni says, patting my shoulder.

I go over to the small table and drink my now tepid tea. As I put the cup down, I upset the platter of fruit and bread. I curse and rush to pick the mess up.

"What are you doing?" Cosra demands with angry eyes.

"Pardon?"

"What are you doing?" she repeats, kneeling near me.

"I'm sorry for the mess." I try to laugh as I gather the bread and fruit off the floor. I dump my handfuls back on the plate. "I've always been a tad clumsy."

Cosra picks up the crumbs and dumps them into her bucket of ashes. Under her breath, she mutters, "You are an odd one." Then louder, she says, "The steward will have my head if he hears you cleaned up." She scowls.

"I have hands and know how to use them," I say, trying to placate her.

Her thin lips twist. "Is this how they do it in Fernwald? Your sister had me whipped. You'll have me punished."

Her words shock me to the core. "What?" Alanna wouldn't. She would never have... Cosra isn't old – possibly in her mid-twenties – but she's worked most of her life. For a moment, I feel shame at the ease at which I've lived.

Cosra reties the handkerchief around her hair, sniffing defensively. "I didn't get her dresses cleaned properly." She sits back on her haunches and evaluates me. "This surprises you. Maybe you didn't know your sister all that well. She made many enemies with her attitude."

Rather than being offended at Cosra's bluntness, I use it as an opportunity to learn. "Enemies? Enemies that wanted her dead?"

Cosra stands abruptly, and I become aware that I've overlooked a possible source of information. The princes had questioned the staff but had the staff been honest? Indecision flashes across her face before she comes to a decision. "You should know that there are some who would rather have a different king. Two princes supported by very different powers. Maybe you should ask the king's brothers if you want to know what happened to your sister."

My blood runs cold as she grabs her bucket and leaves me to my thoughts. When Torin fetches me, I quickly tell him what

Cosra said.

He rubs his chin. "I will see what I can uncover talking to the soldiers. There is no great love for the king. Not when he leaves his young queen to do his work."

I'm surprised by the resentment in Torin's tone, but should I be? It's true that the moment I became Queen of Tyre that Kel has passed a number of responsibilities onto me.

When I arrive at the Council's chambers, I note Kei and Kol sitting at opposite sides of the table. The king's chair is empty as usual. When I sit, though, I make a conscious decision and take King Kel's seat.

Count Andes is aghast. "Your Majesty," he begins.

"Today," I say in a loud voice, "I would like to deal with obsoleting slavery in Tyre." I note which lords bristle and which ones lean forward. Both Kei and Kol are stoic in their seats. "All other issues will be tabled until we reach an agreement."

Lord Milas, an elderly sort with a long beard, starts to stammer, "T-this is most unusual, Your Majesty. W-we have agendas—"

"Explain your agenda to the women and men and children bound by nothing more than a piece of paper." I refuse to stand down. "For years, Fernwald has governed without the use of primitive means. It is time for Tyre to do the same."

"And who will tend my crops?" asks one lord.

"Do you mean to deprive me of my assets?" asks another.

I level everyone with a glare. "People are not assets. You will tend to your crops by offering wages or an exchange as lords have done in other kingdoms." I raise my hand for silence. "What is a person's worth to you, my lords?" Torin hands me a pouch which I'd instructed him to carry for me earlier. I pull out a gold coin from Fernwald. "One of these?" I toss it on the table. Several men stare at it greedily. "Two? Three?" I stand up, and Kei and Kol hastily get to their feet. "If I have to buy every person you've enslaved with Fernwald's wealth, I will. And I will set them free. But tell me, gentlemen, how it would look that a woman had to cover the mismanagement of your estates. Among you, the major lands of Tyre are covered. If you cannot make your vassals obey the royal edict which will be issues shortly, then shame on you and your poor governance. Your lands belong to you by the king's justice and will." I lift my chin and hope that I look regal. "I do hope the lords of Tyre do not need a mere woman to tell them how to manage their lands."

I know I've pricked their pride. Kei's lips twitch, but Kol stares at me with wide eyes. I'm being reckless, but Cosra's words to me earlier have made me so. I will find out who these factions are. I owe Alanna that much.

X: WITHOUT LOVE

In the mornings, if King Kel is feeling particularly interested in how I'm handling his affairs, he has breakfast with me.

I watch him dip a piece of golden bread into honey. After eating the bite, he licks his fingers. He manages to look good while doing that. "I heard from Kol that you took the Council by storm. Aren't they boring and stodgy?"

His question, and his smile is kind. I smile back. "Thank you, my lord." Formal. The edict abolishing slavery in Tyre was issued yesterday. There's a sense of pride in that accomplishment.

"We make a fabulous team, Ilyria." Kel's handsome face is content. "We are very compatible in that regard. But there is one area which you may need to tend to. The ladies of the court. You will have women who will serve you, and you will want to get that into order. But there is another matter to deal with."

"Oh?" The thought of dealing with court ladies makes me shudder internally.

"It's Kei's mother." At my start, his lips twitch. "Yes, she's still alive. You know, when she had that affair with my father, my mother was still alive. Of course, she expected to become the Royal Concubine. Who would've known that Father would've seen Kol's mother?" He takes my silence for connivance. "She only comes to court on occasion, but it is up to you whether or not she will be welcome here."

"Do you have a preference?" I never thought myself skilled in court politics, and yet I find myself playing them constantly these days. It's... tiring.

King Kel shrugs. “It matters not. Tassia isn’t pleased with her, of course.”

That doesn’t surprise me. Upholding Kei’s mother would undermine Kol’s place in the line of succession. Since Tassia probably intends for her future sons to sit on the throne, she wouldn’t support anything that might legitimize Kei in the eyes of the people. “Then I will decide based on the merit of her presence.”

Kei has avoided me since my coronation, but I frequently find him looking at me during meetings and state dinners. He does it surreptitiously, usually when he’s walking close to the king or about to leave. I have wondered frequently how Kei’s mother was treated at court

Kol’s comments and Cosra’s words about Alanna weigh on my mind. She was my sister: lovely and flawed, good and bad, kind and cruel. It would be easy to criticize her actions or assume the worst, but that would be unjust. I do not know what she was thrown into or what forces worked against her. I don’t know if her actions were deliberately cruel or whether she reacted defensively. She came here without her personal guard because she found him stuffy and insisted that Tyre’s royal guards would keep her safe. Goodness knows what happened when she met Lady Tassia.

As if my thoughts of her conjure her, Lady Tassia enters with a dismayed look. Our paths rarely cross since I’m normally cooped up in meetings. And when we do see each other, we give each other wide berths.

“My dear,” she says to Kel, “I did hope you would breakfast with me.” She pouts while running her finger along his collar. “I’m starting to think you don’t fancy me at all.”

A flash of irritation crosses Kel’s face. “Tassia, I’m hardly neglecting you. Ilyria and I are discussing state matters.”

I say nothing. Tassia doesn’t bother to hide her irritation. “You can discuss those matters with me.”

“She is Queen, Tassia. Not you,” he reminds her. “Do not forget your position in my court.”

Tassia blanches, her eyes growing so wide that I can see the whites all around. She changes tactics, bursting into tears. "How can you be so cruel to me? Just last night, you held me in your arms and said you loved me."

Kel softens. "Come now, don't cry. There are things you aren't privy to, Tassia, because they don't concern you." He stands up to console her. "How about this? Shall we journey into town and see what wares we can find?" When she sniffles and nods, Kel turns to me. "Ilyria, there's an issue with one of the port towns. Istur. Would you sit in on the morning meeting and see if you can sort the problem out?"

"Of course." I think the Council has gotten used to my presence (and the king's absence) by now.

"You're a wonder," Kel says to me. "See, Tassia, I have cleared my morning just for you." He gazes at her as she lays a proprietary hand on his shoulder. Tassia is triumphant as she straightens her shoulders.

"How fortunate that your *wife* is so useful," the older woman says, her pale brown eyes on my face. "And I am so glad I can fulfill your other needs."

My face burns. I know exactly what those *other needs* are, and even if I were willing, I doubt I would be Kel's first choice anyway. I wonder if Kel's disappointed in my reservations or relieved. I think the latter.

"My lord, I will take my leave," I say as Kel continues to ignore me. Tassia's beauty, I'm sure, is nothing but blinding. Kol's and Kei's description of Kel – him being almost too kind – is accurate. His heart is easily swayed by beauty. He is fond of me and kind. But there is no desire in his eyes or words. I find him beautiful and handsome, and I could easily love him if it weren't for Tassia.

Torin waits for me outside, patient as ever, and walks me to the Council's chamber. "Alone again?" is his quiet question. His question is rhetorical and a tad sympathetic. He has no love for Tassia either.

Torin had been married years ago when I but a child. His wife had served my mother in her youth. But sadly, like my mother, Torin's wife died in childbirth – and the child with her. Torin's devotion to my care and safety began then. I am a surrogate daughter.

During our walk, Torin fills me in on the particulars. The port town of Istur is raided yearly by "barbarians from the North," and for the past twenty years, the status quo had been to evacuate the town, let them come, and then return in the winter. "They leave before the winter closes the Northern Passage," Torin says, his discussions with guards providing the necessary background I need, "and this is an issue because it costs money to rebuild what is destroyed."

When I enter the room, the lords are waiting, including Kei and Kol, and there is no surprise on their faces. I take my seat at the head of the table. "I have been briefed about the situation in Istur," I say. "What are our options?"

A young lord – Earl of Pollux or something like that – is flush with righteous indignation. "We have to take in the refugees, and we are not compensated by the crown. How are my lands to prosper with such a burden? And what if the barbarians decide Istur is not enough?"

Lord Milas, vocal as ever, tells me, "We can't possibly defend Istur. The way those barbarians fight..."

"Perhaps my brother can shed some light," Kei says with a sneer. "Was your mother not from the North? Does their barbarianism run in the blood?" A chuckle leaves a few of the lords' lips when Kol turns white with anger.

Kol addresses me directly. "It's true my mother was captured from one of the raids, and that she was born in the North," he says to me, his cheeks turning red under my scrutiny. Does he believe I think less of him because of this knowledge?

Truth be told, I didn't know Kol's mother had hailed from the North, but this explains why some prefer Kei's claim as King Kel's heir. Kei's mother is from one of the wealthiest families in Tyre, and he was born before Kol. Kol isn't just the son of a slave; he is half-Northern. In Tyre's eyes, that makes him flawed.

I will explore that issue later. For now, I refuse to let

Kei hijack the meeting to push his agenda. "How is Prince Kol's mother relevant to the situation in Istur now, Prince Kei?" I ask archly, waiting until Kei bows his head in a half-hearted apology. I look around the table. "I thought you asked for the king's counsel because you were concerned for our citizens. Am I wrong?" When no one responds, I say, "While I am no expert on military maneuvers, it takes time to build up a military force. Clearly, Tyre has left no garrison in Istur before, and thus the military presence there is limited at best."

Kol clears his throat. "Your Majesty is correct that there isn't time to send an army to defend Istur. I suggest we evacuate the town as usual and send reinforcements to Pollux."

I tap my fingers on the table for silence. *In any military conflict, evaluate the terrain and use it to your advantage.* Ah, Ronan, I still remember our lessons together. "Does Pollux have enough of a garrison to defend?" I ask. When the lords agree that there is enough to hold for a few days, I suggest, "Let build a muster there. Can the town support additional troops?"

The Earl of Pollux gives me an uneasy smile. "If we have *financial* support from the crown, yes."

It always boils down to money. My response is cool. "Of course." I think of what exists in the coffers, as well as the influx of coin from Fernwald. My dowry on top of Alanna's. Yes, we can support an increased garrison in Pollux. "Send the reinforcements."

Kei crosses his arms on the table. "You want to make a stand next year," he guesses correctly.

"That is the plan."

Some of the lords view me with varying levels of respect. Others are confused. Kei raises his hand to prevent others from speaking prematurely. "Your Majesty, my lands border Pollux. Pollux is rich in grain. We can support the effort in exchange for grain to my ducal lands."

At that offer, other lords step in to assist Pollux, and the relieved expression on the young lord tells me that the impetus from Kei was greatly needed. On our journey to Tyre, I had wanted to trust Kei. "I need more information, Lord Andes. The force we typically see from the North in Istur, and how soon after raiding do they leave. Would you organize that information for me?"

When Lord Andes agrees to my request, I clasp my hands together. "Now then, gentlemen, what else is there on today's agenda?"

XI: THE JEWELRY BOX

I'm surprised when Kei asks for a private audience with me. Cymoni is concerned by the sudden turn and insists on being in the chamber parted by curtains – presumably to listen and observe. I don't think Kei is a danger to me, but Torin approves of this precaution.

When Kei arrives in my private receiving chambers, he observes the curtain and the way Torin looks at him with a small smile. His brown eyes – a shade lighter than Kol's and more faceted than Kel's – shine with undisguised humor.

"You are unlike your sister," Kei says, and I know he bring Alanna up to disarm me.

"Is that a compliment?" I quip. "Wine?"

He shakes his head. "You don't need to be polite or play games. Let's not insult each other."

Cymoni had laid out fruit and wine beforehand. I pop a grape in my mouth and chew thoughtfully. After I swallow, I face Kei directly. "Fine. No games. Why are you here?"

Kei's eyes widen, but he recovers quickly. "You have been absent from the women's chambers," he says.

"You came to me to discuss that?" I watch him flush.

"My mother is at Court," Kei retorts.

Ah, so that is why he is here. He wants to know if I will receive his mother in front of the other ladies. I walk to the window embrasure and stare blindly out.

"While you deal with matters my brother should govern, Tassia rules over the women's chambers." Kei walks over to stand in front of me, his handsome face stiff and unyielding. "I want to know what your stance will be with my mother."

Ironic. He slighted me by withholding information, and now he curries my favor. What made him behave that way? "Why didn't you tell me about Lady Tassia?" I ask, refusing to be baited.

Kei has the grace to flush, but he continues with his indolent air. "That was a mistake," he admits. "I did it out of spite. But that was before I got to know you."

I raise a brow. "Oh, that makes it so much better."

"I must admit, you handled it well."

"I'm glad you approve."

Kei lowers his eyes. "Would it help if I apologized?"

"No." When he's surprised the finality of my tone, I cross my arms. "Whatever you think of me, Kei, is irrelevant. I will judge your mother by her actions alone and not by whatever offense you have done." He blinks. *Don't make enemies even if they are your enemies.* "On the road, when we were attacked, you defended me. I thought there was a chance we would become friends. I wanted to trust you and Kol. I wanted your friendship because I knew I would arrive here without love. But you chose to try and hurt me, and I don't know whether your actions were purely capricious or fueled by something else."

He stammers, "I – I d-didn't—"

"I think at one time, you and Kol were friends." I narrow my eyes. "Torn between court politics, you only had each other. I think, perhaps, you were even close with Kel. And then Kel became king. And you became a pawn to the ambitions of various lords. Think carefully where your loyalties lie, Kei, and think carefully whether or not you think I lack the wit to survive. I may be young, but I'm not an idiot."

Kei is silent for a moment. "I see my brother has married a true queen," he says finally. "I await the queen's justice on the matter of my mother." He bows, and when he straightens, he eyes me strangely. "I wish—" He breaks off and shakes his head. "Your Majesty. I apologize for taking your time." He bows again and leaves.

"That was interesting," Cymoni says, entering from the

curtained area. That sharp mind of hers never misses anything. "You have learned much under your brother's tutelage."

I shrug. "Father used to drag Ronan to meetings all the time. I would hide behind columns and listen."

"I remember that well, poppet."

"Strange. I had these ideas, ambitions, of how I would rule. When I told Ronan, he would tell me that I would make a fine advisor. In fact, he insisted I become his chancellor when he became king. I can hear him, Cymoni. I can hear Ronan's voice. He guides me even though we're apart."

"I know you miss him, but I believe this is your calling," Cymoni says, patting me gently. "You would have been wasted as a forgotten Second Daughter."

Just then, Cosra enters. Her demeanor towards me has softened in the past few days, but I normally see her only in the mornings and evenings. To see her now makes me curious. Her face is guarded as she approaches me. "Your Majesty." From beneath her apron, she pulls out a wooden box.

I gasp, my heart clenching in pain when I recognize the jewelry box I decorated for Alanna as a child. "Where – where did you find that?"

Cosra glances around as if she is concerned we will be overheard. "They cleaned your sister's rooms after she died." When I flinch, her voice grows kinder. "You know I served your sister. She was – not like you."

I manage a nod not trusting myself to speak. Cymoni places a warm hand on my back as I take the box from Cosra.

"This was the only thing Princess Alanna seemed to treasure when I was in her presence. It was the only time her face was kind. They left the dresses, but the orders were to remove everything else."

"On whose orders?" I ask.

"I know not. Whoever orders the Steward of the Court."

Which means someone orchestrated the removal of Alanna's things and asked the steward to take action. But who and why? "Cosra, what do the servants say about Alanna's death?"

Cosra has her own loyalties, and they are not necessarily to me.

Cosra looks me in the eye. "They say that it is easier to remove the heir of a concubine than that of a queen," she says.

And I wonder if Kol or Kei know this.

XII: ALANNA

It isn't until the following day that I take time to look at Alanna's jewelry box. That may seem strange at first, but the truth is that I needed the strength to open it. I waited until I was alone – no Cymoni or Torin to observe, no pages to ask me to sit in on a meeting the king was supposed to attend.

"Alanna, I wish I had been a better sister," I say, the fire my only source of comfort.

My fingers brush over the flowers I had painted years ago. The colors have held up well despite everything. I'm touched that Alanna brought this with her from Fernwald. Of all the things she kept, this is significant.

When I open the box, I see the usual trinkets. A ring my father gifted her at sixteen, the ruby the size of a pearl. A pearl necklace that belonged to my mother. Earrings my brother bought for her when Alanna turned eighteen. A bracelet given to her by King Kel upon the announcement of their engagement.

The velvet lining, once a bright blue, is faded and worn. I try to fix a corner and find myself worrying at a frayed edge. When I push against the roof of the box, I feel an unexpected give. Using a nail, I pry the velvet lining loose.

Beneath the lining, I find a wadded piece of paper filled with crowded script. The writing is a cramped, nervous version of Alanna's usual style.

I pray this box is returned to Fernwald. I am careful in who I trust. I hold my airs. Everyone thinks I am a pampered, spoiled princess. Better to be underestimated than not. Something is wrong here. I dare not trust Kel's brothers. I think one of them is trying to kill me. The steps were not an accident. I hope this box makes it back to Ilyria. She is clever enough to understand. Oh, sister, if only I had your intelligence. I do not think I will last a fortnight.

I stare at my sister's words. When did she write this? There is desperation and fear and resignation. She knew. Alanna knew someone was trying to kill her. Once more, I am assuaged by images of Alanna gasping, dying from the poison running through her veins. Despite all her airs, she tried to send a message to me. Without a personal guard, she didn't know whom to trust. Without a friend, she had barricaded herself emotionally by being vindictive and cruel. Desperate measures by a desperate princess.

I hold the paper in numb fingers. This is a precious message. She had not trusted messengers to reach me, but something – or someone – had made her wary. How long did she live in fear? Did she know as the poison crept through her veins who had sided against her?

Kei and Kol. She feared them, but why? *The steps were not an accident.* What happened?

The note is too dangerous to keep and too dangerous to say aloud. With Cymoni and Torin guarding my food and watching others, I am harder to kill, but it is not impossible. So far, I haven't seen anything to make me wary, but my actions have been bold, brash. What if my would-be murderers are watching me and biding their time?

As evening approaches, I collect myself. The king is holding court to celebrate the fall harvest, and as queen, I am to attend.

Cymoni dresses me in a new gown made from my sister's dresses. The current fashion here are pastel hues: pink, light blue, a hint of green. The silks Alanna had chosen, however, are bold and vibrant – rich jewel tones of green, blue, and red. The silk shimmers subtly in the light, and rather than being wisps of cloth, the material is more substantial. I will never have Alanna's beautiful form and grace, but the tailored dress fits me well. Cymoni has taken the flowy dresses of Tyre and added structured panels of silk. The skirt forms an A-line that flatters me and hides my lack of curves. Rather than a deep neckline, the bosom modestly displays my collarbone without revealing too much skin.

"Cymoni, you are wasted as my nurse and should be a dressmaker," I say.

The older woman laughs. "Do you think I spent all my time watching and caring for you? How many dresses did you tear that I had to mend so your father would not scold you? I learned a thing or two, child."

When Torin arrives, I fill him in on Alanna's note. His weathered face turns graver. "Will you do a bit of digging, Torin? Find out about the steps incident?"

Torin's gift is that common soldiers like and trust him. He has an honest heart that wins over even the grumpiest of men. "I will," he promises, "but this means you must take care. I never worked with your sister, but forgive me for saying, she was careless. She should never have come here without someone from Fernwald she could trust."

Torin escorts me to the main hall where I find the king waiting for me.

"My queen," King Kel says with a gallant nod of his head. Behind him, Lady Tassia's curtsey barely passes for respect. I ignore her. The king takes in my attire. "You look well." This is his first compliment to me.

I take the king's proffered arm, and when the herald announces us, we walk in together – King and Queen of Tyre. Lady Tassia must walk ten steps behind not just us, but the king's heirs, Kei and Kol. I try not to feel a twinge of spiteful glee.

On the dais, the king and I observe our court before we sit. Behind our two thrones, Tassia has a small stool – unobtrusive and hidden. The stool is only a courtesy as she is not allowed to meddle in court affairs.

King Kel gestures to his brother Kei, and the prince makes his way warily over. "Your Majesties." Kei is all courtesy.

I look at Kei with a different eye. Alanna's letter is fresh in my mind, and I wish I could read Kei better.

"I understand your Lady Mother is here," Kel says as if he doesn't know it for a fact.

Kei bows. "Yes, my Lord King. Should I bring her?"

Kel turns his rich brown eyes to me, his oval face handsome and solemn. I don't think he knows what I plan to do either. "Please present her to my queen."

An older woman – her face still showing traces of handsome beauty – steps forward to take Kei's extended hand. She is dressed in pale yellow, and the youthful cut of the dress is at odds with her age. The color adds a sallow look to her skin. Her eyes, however, are striking. Kei has her eyes – large, well-spaced, and wide with a haughty tilt.

"May I present my mother, Lady Fleura of Taeran," Kei says in a stiff voice. There is unhappiness in his face.

Before I react, I wonder about Kei's relationship with his mother. He holds her hand as if she carries a disease. Despite the haughty expression on her face, I see fear and shame. She gave herself to the king but was supplanted by a woman from the North, and her only saving grace is her son's lineage. Royal bastard he may be, but at least he does not have Northern blood. That is what some of the lords whisper in shadows.

I stand, and a ripple of curiosity floats through the room. I go down a few steps. "Lady, rise," I say in a firm voice. "My husband's brother's mother is kin to me and mine. Be welcome at our court."

In one stroke, I have welcomed the mother of a man who might want me dead. Kei and I cross glances, and I note Kol's sudden pallor. I have made my move. Now I need to see what happens next.

XIII: STEPS

I can no longer avoid the women's chambers – after all, I am Queen of Tyre. They are under my management. (I do wonder what Kel does with his spare time. Perhaps he'll tell me if I ask him someday, but I'll be honest that I'm not eager to hear about his escapades with Tassia.)

When I arrive, I'm greeted by none other than Lady Tassia. Honestly, I'm surprised she isn't with my husband. But then again, I had told Kel I would be here today, and he probably told Tassia. My smile is a tad stilted, but with Cymoni at my back, my courage is bolstered. As the ladies rise hastily, I note Lady Tassia's slow rise.

Cymoni, however, uses her best grumpy voice to point out Tassia's actions. "Here, here! This is your queen, and you rise like you're older than me. I don't remember ladies being so lazy in Fernwald. What is it, Lady Tassia? You sit there as if you think you might be a queen yourself! Make way, make way!"

The other ladies gasp, but Tassia is white with rage. With jerky movements, she moves away from the window embrasure, and I take her spot. Cymoni hands me a piece of fine linen where the outlines of a purple flower have been started. I hate stitching. The ladies adjust themselves accordingly, with Tassia taking the seat closest to me.

With the sun's filtered light, the solar is almost too warm. Slowly, the ladies begin to talk.

"I hear that the harvest will be good this year," says Lady Lisel, a myopic woman with good intentions.

I'm still staring at my stitching. I hate stitching flowers. I don't want them on my dresses. Before I can say something, the parting curtain admits Lady Fleura. Kei's mother has come to see how welcome she is at my court.

"Oh, make room for Prince Kei's mother," I say.

"Your Majesty is very kind," Tassia says, and I know she is being unkind with her words.

Lady Fleura and Lady Tassia cross gazes – they are clearly not friends – and I wonder how many times the Court has been ripped apart by the whims of people. The ladies must view me as a curiosity. On one side, I have freed the slaves, strengthening Kol's claim as Heir Apparent. On the other, I have welcomed Kei's mother to my court.

As the women take up their stitching and embroidery, Tassia issues the first attack. "Now that the king has a queen and a concubine, there may be an uncontested heir or two next year." Pretending to engage me in a friendly conversation, Tassia explains, "Prince Kei was only made a prince by the whim of his late father, the old king."

Fleura stiffens. "Kei has had the same education as King Kel and Prince Kol," she says sharply. "And my kin rule the north."

"Which is why our king needs an undisputed heir," Tassia responds. "Not one whose history or blood is tainted."

Cymoni snorts in an unladylike fashion. "You ladies have a queen now. It is her opinion that matters."

The women look at me and laugh nervously. I lift my chin and in a calm voice reply, "My husband's late father gave his three sons an equal education because he loved them equally." I have no idea if this is true, but it sounds good. "Now it is up to our king, my husband, to decide the new order." I rather enjoy saying 'my husband' in front of Tassia.

My point has been made and the women quiet, but just as I being to fear that they would notice my lack of progress on my flower, a young page runs in, breathless.

"Your Majesty," he says in his high voice, giving me a wobbly bow. "The King has a headache and asks you attend the trade discussion in his stead."

Normally, the thought of attending another meeting is not

one I would greet with glee, but right now I am grateful beyond measure.

"Oh, I shall attend the Council right away," I state. "Please let the lords know I shall be there shortly."

Tassia also stands. "Ah, I shall attend my lord," she says with a sly look. "I frequently ease his headaches with my voice."

I try not to laugh at the absurdity of her statement. As Cymoni and I head towards the Council's chambers, I realize I am without my crown. I send Cymoni to fetch it for me while I wait for Torin to meet me near the steps to the women's solar.

After a few minutes, I note a robed cleric, his hood pulled forward, climbing the steps with a large pile of books in his arms. I move aside to give him space, but when he passes me, the books fall to the floor. Distracted, I don't see the hand slamming into my back.

And as I topple forward, I remember Alanna's words. *The steps were not an accident.*

I think I scream. There is pain and then darkness.

XIV: AWARENESS

Someone applies a cold compress to my forehead when I groan. My body hurts and I have a wicked headache.

"Gently, gently." The voice is warm and soothing. And male. Not Cymoni.

My eyes open and focus slowly. "Kel," I croak.

The king peers at me worriedly before grabbing a cup of water. He urges me to sip, and after I obediently drink a little, he sighs. "You didn't break any bones, but you've been unconscious for a while."

Has he been tending to me all this time? I stare at him in confusion. "What happened?" My voice is a raspy whisper.

"Someone pushed you," Kol says, appearing in my line of vision. His hands clench and unclench. "I only heard your scream. When I found you, you were – alone."

I have a vague memory of being pushed. "I didn't see anyone."

"All that matters is that you are well and healing remarkably well," Kel says with a cheerful smile.

"She could have died," Kol snaps in a tight voice. "We should have more guards with her! Why didn't we learn from what happened to her sister?"

"That's enough," Kel growls at his younger brother.

I close my eyes briefly. "What happened to Alanna? Someone pushed her too?"

"Yes, but she didn't fall as far as you." Kel lowers his head. "A handful of steps. I thought she made it up for attention." He pats my hand awkwardly. "Torin and Cymoni are questioning people.

They should be here soon. For now, rest and heal."

"Have you been here tending to me this entire time?" I ask.

Kel grows embarrassed. "I'm aware that we—haven't connected—but you are my queen. Kol has been here too."

When I look at the prince, he turns red. I'm filled with anxious pleasure, but then I remember that they are two handsome young men, and I am very plain.

Kel fidgets in his seat. "Ah, brother, would you stay with her until her personal guard returns?"

The air cools a bit, but Kol's face betrays nothing. "Of course."

The king pats my hand again. "I will visit you this evening to be sure you feel better."

After his brother leaves, Kol approaches my bed. "Some of your color has returned," he says. "When I found you, you were so pale that I thought—" He breaks off, clearing his throat. His deep brown eyes search my face as he takes the seat that his brother had just vacated. "We haven't talked much since… I want to earn your trust, Ilyria. I swear to you that I will protect you with my life and my sword." He grabs my hand earnestly.

And that's how Kei finds us. I snatch my hand back, my face warm. I've done nothing wrong, so why do I feel guilty?

Kei continues to look at Kol as he says, "The king was so good as to inform me that our queen was awake. Our people have been besides themselves in despair. I want you to know that I will conduct my own investigation into the matter."

"Did anyone investigate when my sister was pushed?"

Silence greets my question. Of course, no one investigated. The king himself thought she did for attention. Kei clears his throat. "There was an inquiry, but we found nothing amiss. Kol was in charge of it."

Prince Kol's head dips to his chin. "No one saw anything. She was relatively unharmed. A sprained wrist." A flash of guilt.

"Someone pushed me," I state flatly.

Kei nods. "That is clear. Two sisters falling down steps cannot be coincidental." When I glare, he flushes. "Forgive me. I didn't mean to sound flippant." Concern stamps his face. "I was worried about you."

I think about these two princes who led me here under the impression that Lady Tassia did not exist. Their actions were hurtful, and it was meant to be. I cannot allow myself to be sentimental because of their concern, and I must be careful of my trust. "Were you? Both of you?" Surprised by my question, they rock back on their heels as I continue, "Now you two must forgive me if I am wary of your sincerity. I believed *in* both of you once. And I want to believe. But I find it hard to believe that in the past few weeks I've suddenly earned your loyalty." Alanna's letter hardens my heart a little. Perhaps she trusted them. Perhaps she became cautious too late.

Kei bows deeply. "My queen." His eyes, almond-shaped and expressive in his handsome face, linger on me. "I owe you an explanation. We both do."

"Now is not the time," Kol protests. "She's hurt and needs to rest."

"I am well enough to hear this," I say in a firm voice despite my headache.

"When Princess Alanna came here, the kingdom was excited. Your sister is – was beautiful and graceful," Kei begins. "But she clashed with everyone. She was here less than a week before she began to argue with the servants. After her death, when Kel made it obvious he intended the alliance between Fernwald and Tyre to hold and marry you, Tassia came to us and told us what she knew of you. We believed her. I admit we were wrong to do so."

"At least you two were in agreement," I observe wryly.

The younger prince bites his lower lip, shifting from one foot to another. There is so much uncertainty in his face. "I will find out who tried to kill you," he finally says with emotion. "I swear it."

I want to believe him, but what if he made the same promises to Alanna? What if Kei made pretty speeches? I only have Kei's word that Alanna was difficult, although Cosra had intimated the same. Perhaps my suspicions show on my face because Kol's eyes, guileless as a fawn, fill with sorrow.

Kei bends a knee. "I sometimes wonder if Kel knows what he has," he says almost to himself. "My queen." After inclining his head, he looks at me one more time before bouncing to his feet and leaving.

And I can't explain why my heart skips a beat.

XV: CALAMITY

It's a rare thing for Kel to attend Council, but he does just that this morning. With my morning free, I spend it in the castle's vast library. There are anthologies to explore, histories to uncover, and tales to learn. I consider the libraries in Fernwald to be better than average, but I've never had the opportunity to see history through the eyes of a different land.

I find the old librarian to be kind and helpful. "I can't seem to find history books that talk about the First Daughter and her sisters," I tell him.

The old man is surprised by my request. "For a while, our stories were relayed orally," he explains. "Our earliest histories were passed down, parent to child, before being recorded. But, if you give me some time, I will have books delivered to Your Majesty of what exists. I'm afraid those books are buried in the vaults of our library. Is there anything, in particular, you are looking for?"

"I'm looking at how Tyre recorded the story of the First Daughter," I reply. "But I'm also interested in the history of the North. Tyre has had more encounters with them than Fernwald. Surely within these great walls, there is some information about them."

The old man starts at my request, but then a sly smile appears on his face. "I see we have a true scholar among us." He walks over to a worn book on a pedestal. "This is a record of the king's family. You may find some interest in there, and I will get back to Your Majesty on the other matter."

I spend a few hours learning about Kel's family. The records are scrupulous, accounting for every birth and death, and providing detail in between. Kel's father, King Ayd, had been the youngest of three sons. His brothers had died young and left him the sole heir. Based on the records, King Ayd's queen was still alive when he took Kol's mother as his concubine. Rather than a full family name, Kol's mother is listed as 'Alia of Asterin'.

What I find curious is that after Alia's death, King Ayd had Kei's birth recorded and written in the book. Bastards are not always recognized by their parents. I remember Kei's mother emphasizing that Kei, Kol, and Kel received the same education. Did Alia's death spur the king to take responsibility? Or was Alia's manner of death a catalyst? Perhaps the lords were unhappy with a fleeing concubine.

Torin, who had been standing at the entrance of the library, comes to fetch me. "The king requests your presence," he tells me, solemn as usual.

I thank the librarian after reminding him of the research I wish him to conduct. When I reach the king's receiving room, Kel is there, his lips stained with wine and curved in a smile, and so is Lady Tassia. The latter is resplendent in pale yellow silk. I wonder how large her wardrobe budget is. "My dear," Kel says, gallant as always. "I have an announcement to make, which is why I invited you and Tassia."

Tassia pours wine for all of us. "Should I get the princes?" she asks in a fake, sweet voice.

Kel nods, and after Tassia leaves, says to me, "It's about the succession and who I choose as my heir until I have a son." He hands me my wine glass.

I stare at the ruby-colored liquid and set the cup down. Flagging a page, I say, "Would you have tea brought to me instead?"

The page bows twice in his eagerness to comply, and Kel surprises me by laughing indulgently. "You are a favorite among my staff, I hear. And the common folks love you, too. My Council tells me I should be more like you." He drains his cup and takes mine. "Fine wine should never go to waste."

I smile and wonder if he should drink so much. "And your

Council approves of your decision?"

"Unanimously." He sits in a plushy chair and regards me with a strange seriousness. "Ilyria, I have taken you for granted. As you may have guessed, I am not… I never wanted to be king. My dream would have been to be a pampered prince, enjoying all the privileges with little work." His deep eyes wait for a reaction, but I show none. "You are an intriguing young woman, and I hope we do become friends. There are many marriages built on much less."

At his gesture, I sit across from him. "I know."

"Perhaps it was unwise to take a concubine before I got formally married," he says with a sigh. "Tassia isn't suitable as a king's consort. She's the daughter of a lesser lord, bastard born, who only inherited because his brother died." Kel's lips twist. "The Council despises her. They find her temperamental."

I suspect her temperament is part of her allure for Kel, but I remain quiet. Kel has never opened up to me before, and for the sake of the kingdom, I continue to listen.

"And she is. But I think it is best to not muddle the line of succession. Our firstborn son should have an undisputed claim to the throne."

A sense of unease fills me. While I have requested the Right of Mourning, Kel could revoke that right, though it would be unchivalrous to do so.

"If Tassia were to have a child before you do…" He trails off and his lips pout as he considers potential ramifications. "It's why I have decided to name my rightful heir until I have a son. It is the right thing to do." He drinks from my cup deeply, and the alcohol loosens his tongue further. "I admit, Ilyria, when I first saw you, I did not think you could be Alanna's sister. Alanna was exquisite."

I don't express pain or dismay at his words. I've heard them before. Alanna is – was – beautiful, elegant, and graceful. Poets tried to capture her beauty in words. No one tried to capture my looks in words.

"But you are of different mettle, and I admit that you are likable." Kel salutes me with his cup.

Not the most romantic of lines, but again, I am not

romantic. I've always known that no man would ever look at me and fall instantly in love.

The page returns with a maid carrying my tea. Cymoni winks at me by the doorway to assure me she oversaw the operation. I thank them and blow on the tea to cool it.

Tassia returns with Kol and Kei, both princes equally befuddled to see their brother with his wife and concubine all in one room. I wrap my fingers gently around my teacup.

Tassia's eyes narrow. "You don't care for wine?" Her question is sharp and accusatory.

"Don't worry, my dear, I'm finishing her cup," Kel says easily.

Tassia sucks in her breath, and as Kel drains the last of my wine, she slaps the cup away. "No! No! Don't!" she shrieks, her face pale and filled with horror. "No!"

The cup clatters to the floor and rolls to Kei's feet. We stare at Tassia in consternation, but we never get a chance to ask her why she screamed. Kel doubles over with a cry, and Tassia grabs him with icy fingers.

"No! My lord!" she cries as he looks at her with growing comprehension.

"You," he gasps. He coughs and blood spurts from his mouth.

"Kel!" Kol cries, and both brothers rush to the stricken king.

But Kel pushes Tassia away with sudden ferocity and turns his wounded eyes on me. "Too soon," he chokes out. "Ilyria." He reaches for me, and I'm compelled to take his hand as he falls to his knees.

Kei snarls, grabbing Tassia by the throat. "What have you done, you whore?!" he shouts, his vicelike grip tightening brutally.

But my attention is on my husband, a man I barely know. Kel pulls my head to his lips. "You, Ilyria. You are my chosen heir."

XVI: WIDOWED

"Don't speak," I urge him. "Get the physician!" My eyes meet Cymoni's. Torin has drawn his sword and guards the door. Cymoni nods and runs, and I hear her authoritative shouts down the hall.

"No, no, I must tell you," Kel manages to say, more blood welling on his lips.

"Kel," Kei says with a sudden sob. He lets Tassia go, and the woman falls to her knees to cry bitterly.

Kel is now on his back, Kol holding one hand while I hold the other. "Ilyria," the king wheezes, "I name you Regent and Queen of Tyre. You must choose the next king. Choose… between Kei and Kol. I wish—" He breaks off and spasms in pain. "Kol. Kei. Sorry. Sorry. Failed. Brother."

"The physician will be here soon. Just hold on," Kol pleads, tears in brown eyes that mirror his oldest brother. "Kel, forgive me for being angry. I'm sorry. I swear I'll do better."

Kei kneels beside me, and the king's eyes flicker to him. "Kel, you can't die," Kei blurts. He doesn't hide his tears as they slide down his tanned cheeks.

"Ilyria is Queen. I grant her," Kel wheezes, "all authority... to choose... the next king. Ily... For...give... wife." His eyes roll back as his body convulses violently. More blood bubbles from his mouth and the sounds he emits are garbled and horrific. His eyes close. And then he is still. Too still. The most handsome man I've ever laid eyes on…is dead. With a free hand, I brush his dark brown hair back from his face. In death, the lines of his face relaxed and pain-free, he barely looks older than me.

"No!" Tassia wails. "This wasn't the plan!"

Kol bends his head, sobbing as he holds on to Kel's hand. But Kei's face goes from grief to fury. He springs to his feet and grabs Tassia by her hair. "Murderer! Whore!" he shouts.

Tassia's eyes widen. "Kei, I made a mistake! Just listen to me, please! We—" She breaks off and winces when Kei yanks her head back hard.

The shiny dagger Kei pulls from his boot moves too fast for anyone to stop as he slams the blade below the ribcage and up. Tassia gasps, eyes wide and mouth open, as the force lifts her off her feet briefly. The light fades from her eyes as Kei pushes her back. She is dead before she hits the floor.

"W-what have you done?" Kol cries.

"She murdered our brother!" Kei screams as he holds his bloody dagger. Red drops drip to the floor. "She meant to kill Ilyria!"

The violence overwhelms me as I kneel beside Kel's body. Dimly, I'm aware of Torin pushing the royal physician through, I'm aware of the physician checking the king's body. But I'm incapable of reacting or moving.

"Your Majesty," the physician asks me in a trembling voice, "did you drink any of the wine?"

I shake my head, closing my eyes. I need to take control of the situation. "My husband has been murdered," I manage to say. My voice is shaky, but I force myself to go on. "Prince Kei, you have executed a woman without trial. I will rule on your actions later." I turn to the men by the door being held back by Torin alone. "By the king and the will of the Council, I have been named Regent and Queen in the interim. Prince Kei, return to your quarters until I summon you." I wait for the prince to meet my eyes. I expect anger or resistance. I get neither.

"My queen," he whispers, bowing. He wipes the tears on his face and leaves the room.

"Prince Kol, please assemble the Council." The younger prince rises to his feet slowly. "Kol, are you present?"

"Yes, Your Majesty."

Not 'my queen' then. I take note of his words. "Cymoni,

stay here until the physician has made arrangements for the—my husband's body." I take a moment to look at Tassia's pitiful form. *Remember those who have crossed you and ask why. Think about what made this person act that way.* Ronan reminds me that I now have another mystery to solve. "Cymoni, will you..." I trail off as I gesture towards Tassia. Cymoni is not a weak-kneed woman. She takes her duties as my nursemaid and protector seriously. I trust her implicitly.

Torin escorts me to the Council's chambers where the lords have assembled in haste. Kei is absent since I've sent him to his room, but Kol is there, grief-stricken but composed.

My legs feel unsteady as I stand before the Council. Count Andes dabs his eyes with a lace kerchief before he announces, "By the will of the king, all hail Queen Ilyria of Tyre! The Council hereby recognizes Queen Ilyria as Regent and Queen for the next twelve months." He unfurls a signed document. "It was the late king's request that his Queen decide whether Prince Kei or Prince Kol should be the next King of Tyre in the event he died without an heir of his body." With unnecessary decorum, the count hands me the document.

I read Kel's will carefully and wonder if he suspected something. Alanna feared for her life. Did Kel? And yet, he died by Tassia's hand – by poison which was likely meant for me. In that moment, I understand all too well why Kel left this task to me. He couldn't choose between his brothers because he loved them equally.

Kol refuses to look at me, and I sense something – resentment or anger – from him. A breath to steady myself before I speak. "My lords, today our king was murdered—"

"By the Royal Concubine," a lord sneers. "A woman of no status and no dignity."

"She meant to kill Queen Ilyria," another shouts, as if that justifies everything.

"Did she also kill Princess Alanna?" a third asks.

That is my question as well, but the lords continue to talk and bicker over each other. I listen – Ronan told me to listen when men argue – and observe. The Council is decidedly split between sides that favor Kei or Kol.

"But why is one prince not here?" Count Andes asks me.

I think he knows. The question is for the other lords. "Prince Kei executed Lady Tassia" I raise a hand for quiet. "Let it be recorded that Lady Tassia did not confess to anything. I have confined Prince Kei to his quarters until I can deal with him."

"Her words were damning," Kol states in a harsh tone. "She reacted only when she saw my brother drink from *your* cup."

"Count Andes, I ask that you lead the investigation regarding Lady Tassia," I say, emotional exhaustion taking its toll on me. "Search her rooms." Andes is meticulous, and he favors Kol in the line of succession, but Torin says the man has an honest reputation.

Kel's will gives me the right to rule and govern. I am not allowed to change the laws or cause a war. I am to keep the kingdom stable and choose a successor. I do not miss the addendum Kel penned at the bottom of his will: a wish that I marry the next King of Tyre.

But first, I must bury a man who was my husband. A man I barely knew, but who left me a kingdom. My hands clench on the table. There will be time to grieve for what might have been… later.

XVII: NO TIME TO BREATHE

It is only fair that Kol is present when I talk to Kei. Torin guards my back silently with grim focus. Kei has been under "house arrest" (and I use that term loosely) for several days. Now that Kel has been entombed near my sister's body, I find time to deal with Kei.

"I executed a traitor," Kei tells me with a stiff back, his eyes flashing. In the privacy of the chamber, he is direct and resolute.

"That was not your call," I point out. "I'm not saying this because I care about titles or who has the right to execute a person. I'm saying this because Tassia could have provided more information."

Kei's eyes are a lighter shade of brown than Kol's. Where Kel was beautiful, Kei is handsome with his square jawline and fine cheekbones. He is every inch an aristocrat. "Tassia was trying to kill you! For that alone she deserved to die!"

In a low voice, Kol finally speaks, "Tassia didn't care about Alanna."

His half-brother snorts. "Of course not. Alanna wasn't a threat to Tassia's power." Kei looks at me. "You are – or were. The fact that Kel left you the throne is proof enough. We all saw how you handled yourself in meetings. You're clever and intelligent and strong when you need to be. Tassia wanted you gone. Andes will tell you the same when he reports to you."

I tap my foot lightly. "I find it strange that Tassia was threatened by me." I speak quietly, not expecting a response.

"Why?" Kol tilts his head, eyes guileless. "Kel was beginning to admire you."

He was in love with his concubine. I hold my tongue because now is not the time for bitter words. "That isn't enough for a woman to want me dead." I shake my head. "There must have been something more, and without her, the truth may be elusive. Don't you see that, Kei?"

"I would have killed her for trying to harm you," Kei says to my startled face. "I regret you won't have your answers, but I cannot regret my action. She could have killed you, Ilyria."

I'm a tad confused by Kei's words, but I push that aside. "I am not from Tyre. Your kingdom is being ruled by a foreign woman, and I can't do this alone. Kei. Kol. I need both of you to help me. Most of the lords follow one of you. Yes, maybe some of them like me. Yes, maybe the people like me. But that isn't enough when it comes to ruling a kingdom."

Kei steps towards me but stops when Torin warns him off. Barely masking a scowl, he says, "I am your loyal subject. Ilyria, may we speak privately?"

"Absolutely not," Kol snarls in a quiet, vicious tone.

Kei looks at his younger brother. "You suspect me?" He pretends to be hurt.

"I won't let you seduce your way to a throne, brother."

It takes me a few minutes to register what Kol is implying, and once I do understand it, I give myself a mental kick. Kei and Kol. I can't trust either of them to be honest with me. They may help me with the kingdom, but I'll never know if their motives are true. Once again, I am alone in this endeavor. Every action of theirs must be suspect.

I wish I could tell them how lonely, how isolating this is. How will I know the real person? How will I judge if they wear masks? "Kei says he's loyal. Are you, Kol?"

"Pardon?"

"Are you loyal to me?" I press.

Kol stiffens. "I was loyal to Kel. I am loyal to his decree that names you Regent and Queen until you choose Kel's successor. So yes, I am loyal to you."

"Rather roundabout way of saying so," Kei mutters.

"She doesn't need to ask," Kol snaps.

"Don't I?" I raise a brow to emphasize my point. "Both of you conspired with Tassia before I arrived, did you not? Don't tell the foreign princess about the Royal Concubine. Let her find out when she arrives here."

"You know why we did that," Kei sputters.

Kol bites his lower lip. "That doesn't make it right, Kei. What we did was wrong, and she didn't deserve that from us."

Kei narrows his eyes. "And who's talking sweetly now, Kol?"

"Enough." I feel older than my nineteen years. "Both of you. You've made one thing clear to me today, so allow me to make myself clear. I may be young, but I'm not a fool. You think you can come here and charm me? All you've done is make me wonder if either of you have ever said an honest word. I don't care what you think of me, and I don't care to be seduced. I will fulfill Kel's will to the best of my ability because that was his wish." I cross my arms. "And Kei. We did verify that Tassia wasn't with child when you killed her. Had she been, that child would have been Kel's true heir."

The color drains from Kei's face.

Kol bends his knee. "My queen," he whispers.

But I am not swayed. "You are dismissed."

XVIII: DECISIONS

Count Andes delivers his report quietly and privately to me. The poison Tassia used is not the same as what killed Alanna based on the symptoms. His investigation yielded a poisoner who supplied the poison recently to Tassia under the belief that it was to be used against rats. The maids told Count Andes that Tassia had become increasingly concerned over my influence over the Council. On top of that, Kel may have inadvertently mentioned to her his intention to change his will to make me his temporary heir.

Alanna's murderer remains elusive. I struggle to accept this because I was certain Tassia was somehow to blame.

I also receive a missive from my brother. By now, the news of Kel's death has reached Fernwald.

Dearest Sister,
I send this by a trusted courier who will deliver it only to Sir Torin. I am both dismayed and distressed by events in Tyre. And yet, I am reassured because I know that the best person in the world is now leading that kingdom.
I know you remain concerned about Alanna. I will give you wisdom here that you already know. There are some mysteries that can never be solved. And there are others that take time. Remember that forcing an issue doesn't always lead to results. Do you remember how we would observe people in the streets or in the castle? If they argued, we would watch and remember. We made stories about them and waited for the truth to enlighten us. Don't be afraid to wait and watch.
Most importantly, guard yourself. Murder makes one bold. Now there

have been two murders. Fear breeds distrust. Distrust breeds paranoia. If one can kill a princess and a king... Do not allow them to make you a target.

Regarding Kel's brothers, I have little advice, but I do trust your judgment. Do not be afraid to question everything.

I wanted to advise you that our scouts have reported movement in the Northern Passage. I remember your words regarding Istur and wonder if they are moving sooner this year. If so, I suggest investigating further to protect your people.

Life here has remained unchanged. I am simply an heir-in-waiting to Father. I miss our time together, but we could not remain children forever.

Your Ever-Loving Brother,
Ronan

It is a precious letter. An important letter where I can hear my brother's voice as if he were beside me. It is very much his style – sparse on details but providing enough information to understand him. His words on Istur bother me. Tyre has scouts as well on the eastern side. Why have we not received any intel?

"Torin, the man whose lands bordered Istur..." I tap my chin.

"Earl of Pollux," Cymoni supplies, grinning when she sees my surprise. "I have eyes and ears."

There is a serendipitous coincidence in Cosra entering my chambers at that moment. "Cosra, a word if you will." I wave her over.

The young woman adjusts her apron with a slight frown and her curtsey is hasty. "Your Majesty?"

"Call me Ilyria in private," I request to her shocked face. "Torin and Cymoni are people who I trust, but I don't know who to trust in Tyre."

Amazed, Cosra asks, "And why would you tell me this?"

I rest my chin on a fist. "Because I think I can trust you to be honest with me. I value honesty greatly."

I wait as she mulls my words. Then, cautiously, she asks, "Why would you trust me?"

"Because you never bothered to hide what you thought of me," I reply. Both Torin and Cymoni nod in agreement.

A flush creeps up Cosra's neck. "I don't dislike you. Not anymore," she admits with reluctance. Then, with a keen eye, Cosra adds, "You want my advice, don't you?"

"I do. What are your thoughts on Prince Kei and Prince Kol?"

Cosra checks to make sure we are alone, and the doors are closed before she responds. "I've only worked in the castle for a few years, but it is widely known that the princes were once best friends. Prince Kei is a planner, and he can be a bit stuffy. He is proud of his heritage on both sides even if he is a bastard. The king made him a prince in his own right and gave him all the titles and honors. He is known to be a good lord and manages his estates well. The other prince is a shyer sort. He is known to be honest and loyal. He's always been a little sad, especially with the way his mother died. I think either would be a fair ruler for Tyre, but you will make half the kingdom angry picking one over the other."

I try not to smile at the flood of information. "Cosra, will you be my friend?"

The woman stares at me. "What are you asking?"

"I don't need a maid. I need a friend. Someone who knows Tyre in and out, someone who will tell me the truth." I grab her flustered hands. "I need someone who will deal with me as a person and not placate me because I'm Queen."

Cosra doesn't pull her hands free. Instead, she evaluates me with a direct, honest look. "Yes. I will try, Your Majesty." When I raise my brow, she corrects herself. "Ilyria."

XIX: INVASION

"What do you mean the North has sent down a force?" I ask stupidly. The moment the words leave my lips, I give myself a mental kick.

In a hastily convened Council, we are minus several lords who've returned to their estates, but that is inconsequential since many of them live in the southern parts of the kingdom. Cosra and Torin are behind me to my left and right respectively – not sitting as they are not Council lords but close, nonetheless. Kei is in the seat to my left, Kol to my right.

Count Andes wrings in his pale hands. "The barbarians swept through Istur. They've never come so early and in such great numbers." A heavy sigh. "Many were killed. There were a few survivors who made their way to Pollux. The word is that the force is more than just a raiding party."

The Earl of Pollux rises to his feet. "My people are farmers, not warriors!"

"Her Majesty's request to send a small force to augment yours has proved fortuitous then," Torin says in his deep voice.

"But it won't be enough, and the muster there won't hold for long if they continue through Tyre," I think out loud.

"I can have four regiments ready with little warning," Kol offers. "My lands are more westerly, but I can organize them quickly."

I make a mental tally, but while I am knowledgeable in many things, I am not a military expert. "How soon can we prepare troops?"

"You intend to send an army to combat the incursion?" Kei

asks, and there is a hardness in his face. I recall that his mother claimed their power base lay in the northern lords and wonder why he hasn't offered to help.

"I do." I carefully place my hands on the table – a move I'd seen my father do when he wanted his lords to listen – and add, "And I intend to go with them." As expected, the Council is not happy with my decision. I let them argue and sputter for a bit. "Listen to me! For years, Tyre has allowed armed men to sweep through Istur without making a stand. They clearly expect us to do nothing! We can't simply send a few men and hope that a slap on the wrist will be a sufficient deterrent."

"But to go yourself…" Andes is shocked.

"I am not Tyre-born, Andes. I can't direct men to protect our kingdom if I'm not there to understand what they must endure. Word must have leaked about King Kel's passing. In their eyes, Tyre appears vulnerable. We can't allow that to stand." I gesture to the Earl of Pollux. "How long can you hold without additional reinforcements?"

"A week or two," the earl says with uncertainty.

I imagine the attackers won't move right away. They would recover, ransack the town, before moving on. So, we had a few weeks at best. "I will take whatever forces we can muster here within a week." Now I flounder. I don't know what it takes to create a military force. I turn to Torin and hope he notices my conundrum.

"With Your Majesty's permission, I will coordinate the forces," Torin booms.

Kei purses his lips before coming to a decision. "I will lend what men I can," he says with a scowl at Kol.

I wonder if they ever played nicely as children. I hold back a sigh and stand, dismissing the Council. Torin leaves to start preparations, and Cosra attends to me to walk me back to my chambers.

"Your Majesty."

I pause and look over my shoulder while Cosra tenses at the voice. Kol walks briskly to me, his young face solemn. "You can't put yourself at risk and go to Istur."

"I don't intend to fight," I say. I mentally roll my eyes as I continue to walk, forcing Kol to jog to catch up to us.

"You don't have to be there," Kol begins. "I can lead the forces."

"No." I don't have to look at him to know he's surprised by my immediate refusal. "It must be me. If I let one of you lead, it will look like favoritism. I can't have that."

"I never knew you cared so much about appearances," Kol mutters.

I hold my tongue. Is there bitterness there? "I'm not, but I'd rather not have the lords of the realm claiming anything. We climb the stairs towards my quarters – I can't help but think how unsuitable gowns are for stair – and realize I haven't shaken my shadow.

"What if something happens to you?" Kol inquires as Cosra opens the doors to my receiving chamber.

I avoid looking at the door that joins this room to the king's chambers as I face Kol. With a gesture, I tell Cosra she can leave, but I know she won't be far. Cosra is a survivor and a fighter. Her trust must be earned. "Nothing will happen to me."

"I will accompany you then," Kol decides. When I open my mouth, he adds, "You cannot forbid it. My men. I have a right to be there."

"Then Kei will want to come," I scowl and cross my arms.

"Even better," Kol says. "You don't want him here stirring trouble."

"How is it that you two used to be friends? What sowed this level of distrust?"

Kol evades my eyes as his throat moves with emotion. "It simply happened... over time. We grew apart, and the more time we spent apart, the more we began to distrust each other."

At this angle, I see so much of Kel in his youngest brother's face. Kol is a blend of Kel's beauty and Kei's handsomeness. How unfortunate for them that I turned out to be so plain. "If both of you come, I won't have you bickering." I rub my temples. "If you can promise me to try, then I will approve it."

"Approve it?" Kol is properly indignant, but his lips twitch.

I give my father's smile – the smile he gives when he's about to be unpleasant. "I don't give a damn that they're your men, and if I have to chain you in a dungeon to stop you, I will."

Noting my demeanor, Kol's hint of humor fades. "And will Kei receive the same warning?" Suspicion in his words.

"Naturally." What an odd question!

"Then I agree." His round dark eyes search my face. "I'm glad Tassia failed to harm you, Ilyria." He takes my hand and kisses the back like a proper gentleman.

But after he's gone, I remember the feel of his lips against my skin.

XX: DISCOVERY

I have never been without Cymoni before, but there the number of people I trust are small, and I need a reliable correspondent to keep me informed. Cymoni stays back to assist Count Andes in my absence. I am vulnerable without her on the road.

With my ad-hoc army, I travel with Kei, Kol, Torin, and Cosra. Cosra, with her streetwise perceptions, speaks little but observes everything. She has become invaluable to my inner circle.

We stop to rest the army and read reports. In the simple tent, Cosra delivers our meal – a rough stew of vegetables and whatever meat the men caught this morning – in plain bowls with a hunk of dry bread. I throw the bread into the stew to soak and continue my reading.

The book is an old one provided by the librarian, but what I find curious is how few creases there are in the binding. It's as if the book hadn't been read much. The words are faded, and due to a lack of care, difficult to read in a number of spots.

"You are reading a lot," Cosra observes rhetorically, taking a seat at the small table. Despite my request to travel simply and lightly, Torin and the princes insisted on certain formalities. "Anything of interest?"

In private, Cosra has adapted to being casual with me, for which I am glad. "This book details the history of Tyre, but it is written very oddly," I say with a frown. "The writer writes almost carelessly."

...tales are told by the victors, are they not? The Tale of the Three Daughters... For where...is the known... Second Daughter... do we... First Daughter or Third? Why would the Third be jealous when her lands were the fair Fernwald? Unless...

When I show Cosra the words, the older woman chews on her lip. "Istur is supposedly close to where the Second Daughter is buried."

My head snaps up. "That's right." I tap the book with a finger. "Our history says the First Man came and fell in love." I wrinkle my nose. "Seriously, was our land populated only with women? Anyway, the three daughters supposedly inherited some of their father's power."

"How else would the First Daughter have fought against her sister's treachery?" Cosra comments.

"Right! But what happened to all that magic?" I ask pointedly. "Before the fight or whatever, the sisters married and had families. Did their children get none of the power whatsoever? No one knows. But look here!" I run my finger across a few fragmented lines. "Here the author implies – in what can be read – that maybe the magic and the tale of the Three Daughters are one and the same."

"You mean more myth than truth?" When I nod, Cosra ponders it. "But why is this important?"

"Well, you yourself said that supposedly the Second Daughter is buried near Istur. Why does the North invade Istur every year? It's a village with some resources, but it is not inherently valuable. That's why Tyre never did much to defend it."

"But the North seem to be intent on doing more now," Cosra says, "much like before."

I tilt my head. "What do you mean like before? The North has brought a large force down before?"

The other woman searches her memory. "Yes. More than twenty years ago. That's how Prince Kol's mother was captured and enslaved. So, it would have to be close to twenty-five years ago. I'm surprised no one told you."

I try to hide my sour expression. Kol may not have mentioned it because it involved his mother. And Kei might have withheld information just to be a jerk.

"You think the events are related? Perhaps you should ask your two princes what they know." Cosra pokes at the stew with a spoon.

I sigh. "They are not *my* princes." I'm about to dig into my stew when I hear a rumble of voices: one deep, one slightly lighter.

Cosra gives me a knowing look as she stands, hands demurely clasped before her.

The tent flap lifts and Kol walks in, carrying his bowl of food. Behind them, Torin rolls his eyes before dropping the flap and returning to guard the entrance.

"Kol," I say. Kol sketches a hasty bow after noting Cosra's presence.

"May I join you?"

I close the book and return it to my stash as I gesture to the open seat in invitation. Kol's rich brown eyes follow me while I put the book away.

"You're reading?" His question is curious, polite.

"Mmmm." I keep my tone noncommittal. "Just trying to learn. Are you familiar with Istur?"

Kol shovels a large spoonful of food in his mouth and nods. Cosra daintily sits next to me as I wait for him to speak. I sometimes forget that Kol is only a few years older than me, and he eats the way my brother did during his growing teen years. Swallowing hastily, Kol says, "Istur is actually north of the duchy I've been granted. Kei's family owns lands further to the west of me."

"I hear the supposed burial site of the Second Daughter is around there."

Kol freezes and then carefully puts his spoon down before answering. "Yes. We'll pass it on the way to Istur."

I smoosh the bread in my bowl, now softened by the liquid, and take a small bite. My thoughts are elsewhere, and I only care that the food is warm and filling as I swallow. "Your mother was from the North." My comment is careful and cautious, but Kol tenses. His hand forms a fist, knuckles blanching in the dim lighting of the tent. "Did she ever tell you about her life before she – came here?"

The prince forces his hand to relax, and, with measured control, he deliberately picks up his spoon and eats again. After a few bites, he finally answers me. "I don't really remember that much. Once, not long before she—" Kol breaks off, his throat moving. "She told me her fondest childhood memory was riding. She had a horse she loved."

Impulsively, I place my hand on his forearm. "I'm sorry to cause you pain," I whisper.

Kol starts at my touch, his eyes pinned on my hand in surprise. When I remove it, his face is vulnerable, gutted. "Have you heard what some of the lords say?" he asks me, not waiting to hear my answer. "They worry I'll see the invaders and long to return home."

Cosra stands. "I can see we may need a second bowl or two," she says with a gesture towards Kol's bowl. "Begging your pardon..."

I know Cosra leaves to give us some semblance of privacy. "Kol, I don't doubt your loyalty to Tyre, but it wouldn't surprise me if you were a little curious about the North."

Kol bites his lip. "Ilyria, I hate how my mother was forced to bear me, but I think she loved me. She must've if she planned to escape with me. As much as I hate the circumstances that allowed my father to trap her here, Tyre is my home. But no woman should be forced to submit. People are not merchandise. And I hate the tradition that allows a king to have a concubine. It devalues the marriage between a king and queen." Kol is almost defiant with his words. "You know, the last time the North came down with a decent force, it was twenty-five years ago. Pollux had more of a military back then. That's how – my mother was captured."

I decide not to reveal my knowledge of this and find myself struggling for words. An awkward silence settles between us, but the quiet is broken by Kol. "I will show you the shrine to the

Second Daughter and where she is supposedly buried," he offers, ducking his head. "If you want."

"Our goal is to get to Istur first, but yes, if it's on the way."

"I loved Kel," Kol says of his dead brother, "but he didn't deserve you." When I look at Kol in surprise, the prince blushes but doesn't back down. "He didn't see what he had, trusting Tassia – no, picking Tassia over you. He didn't value you."

To cover my embarrassment, I try to laugh. "Well, I'm sure it was hard to see me after being surrounded by beautiful women."

Kol's brow furrows. "Tassia may have been beautiful physically, but she was ugly everywhere else. You think so little of yourself." He hesitates, as if debating with himself before coming to a decision. "Ilyria, your eyes… They tell stories by a look. They shine."

I find myself growing hot and cold at once. Can he hear how loudly my heart is beating? I'm beyond flustered by the intensity of his gaze, and I remind myself that I'm still technically in mourning.

The opening of the tent saves me as Cosra returns with more food. If she notices my red face and unsteady breathing, she remains tactfully quiet.

XXI: CROSSROADS

When we arrive at Pollux, we rest the men. It's strange to be so near and far from Fernwald. If I were to head east and cross the water, I would be back home – but is Fernwald home? My life in Fernwald seems like a lifetime ago. I wonder what he thinks of my latest letter.

The scouts sent ahead return, telling us that the Northern group remains camped outside of Istur. Torin assesses the terrain and point out locations which would work towards our advantage. I spend an hour over the maps in an effort to merge military theory to actual implementation. The princes join me towards the end of my study.

"How long would it take to move our men towards Istur?" I ask Torin while Kol and Kei stand on the other side of the table.

"A half day," Torin hedges.

I gnaw on my lip. "What if we were in a rush? How quickly could we move then?"

Kei answers me. "A few hours of heavy riding. You can't run horses to the ground, so you'd have to be sure they were rested enough to handle that." He's puzzled by my questions, but I stay focused on the map.

A sense of anxiety fills me – my instincts say we've wasted enough time on the road and need to move, but the sane thing would be to rest another day here.

"You want to go on?" Kei's tone is incredulous, and I don't blame him.

"We rest for eight hours," I decide, "and then we leave before daybreak."

Torin nods. "I will relay those orders." My faithful Torin: his trust can never be repaid, and I am grateful for his support and solidarity.

"I will assist and get my men prepared," Kol offers. His eyes meet mine briefly before he leaves with Torin.

But Kei is not so easily swayed. "Eight hours? Are you mad?" he asks once we're alone.

"Perhaps. But I have my reasons. In the past, we've played defense. They come; we retreat. This time, I think we should meet them head on."

Kei holds back a retort, closing his eyes for patience. When he opens them, resigned acceptance shines forth. "A better ruler than Kel ever was," he murmurs.

"I know you think I'm crazy, but I have my reasons," I say.

"Not any crazier than falling for your brother's wife," Kei says with a bitter smile.

My brow furrows. I must have heard that incorrectly. I stare at Kei in confusion.

Kei's expressive lips twist. "I remember thinking you weren't much to look at. I thought you would be easy to ignore. But every time you opened your mouth, I wanted to hear more. And now..." He shakes his head with a self-mocking grimace. "I wish I could dislike you, Ilyria. I wish you had come into our lives sooner rather than later." He moves his hand towards my face, but I step back instinctively. His hand drops to his side.

"Kei, I will not grant you the throne just because you spout pretty words." I try to sound firm, but the tremor is noticeable.

"You are wise beyond your years," Kei says quietly. "Don't trust me. Don't trust anyone. Force me to prove myself to you. I assure you that I don't deserve your attention."

With a distracted bow, he leaves me to my thoughts. To say that Kei's behavior is perplexing would be a massive understatement. But I don't have the luxury to consider what his words really mean. Cosra arrives with a hastily gathered meal and urges me to sleep if I can.

My dreams are fitful as faces familiar and unfamiliar

appear: images of Kel's death and Tassia's murder-execution by Kei; Kol kissing my hand; Alanna waving goodbye as she left for Tyre. And then the unfamiliar appear in my dream. A woman whose face is neither young nor old weeps. A person, hooded and heavily cloaked, looms over her. A crescent-shaped knife flashes. Blood spills to the ground.

I wake with a gasp, my heart hammering in my chest, certain that I'm in imminent danger. But I only see Cosra's form near me. I only hear the quiet chatter of men who are awake. And I wonder what my dreams (or nightmares) are trying to tell me.

XXII: THE SHRINE

My sleep isn't enough to feel refreshed, but it will have to do. I doubt any of the men slept more than a few hours. What matters are the horses. With help from the locals in Pollux, the horses have been brushed and tended to, and there's a spring in their step as we leave camp with the barest of provisions. As I observe the men listening to orders, I see the open trust the various men have in Kol and Kei respectively. The princes may lead differently, but it's obvious that they are admired and loved.

Before the sun rises, we are off. "They'll see us coming," Torin guesses as we move at a brisk clip. The wind stings our faces, but I refuse to show discomfort. I can't be seen as weak.

"Did we send messengers out?" I ask.

Torin nods. "As you requested."

Kol maneuvers his horse next to mine, oblivious Cosra's glare when he interposes himself. "You can't be at the front when we engage," he says without preamble.

I deliberately pay him no attention. Torin pretends to find his gloves very interesting.

"Your Majesty," Kol says through gritted teeth. "I'm asking you to stay behind when we get close to Istur. You can't be out in the open."

"You are one of the two heirs to the throne," I say loud enough to be heard over the wind. "Should both of you stay behind with me?"

I don't need to look at him to know that he opposes the idea, but I let him mull it over for a bit. "At the very least, will you have guards around you? If there is a true fight, I can't do my job if

I'm worrying about you." He bites his lip and hesitates. "I need to know you're safe."

Kol's concern seems genuine, but what are the odds that two brothers have developed feelings for me, a person of no great beauty? It would be arrogant and foolish to even think it. Someone as handsome as Kei or as beautiful as Kol could have his pick of women; no one would look at me and consider me equal to their looks. "I have great faith in Torin's ability to keep me safe." I am not lying when I say this: Torin has my complete faith. But I've never been close to combat, and my knowledge comes from books, not real-life experiences.

"The queen will not be near the front lines, Highness," Torin responds gruffly. "There will be a good many men around as well."

Kol doesn't reply, but he continues to ride beside me with a thoughtful expression. "We are not far from the shrine, from the supposed burial site of the Second Daughter," he says after a long silence. "There is a spring there."

"It would be good to rest the horses briefly," I suggest with a side glance at Torin to see if he concurs. A minute nod. Word is spread quickly that we will stop.

A strange anxiety fills me as we get close to the supposed shrine. The moment we stop, I dismount without waiting for anyone to help me. As horses are led to the creek formed by the spring, Kol directs me upstream.

Kei, not to be left behind, walks briskly towards us, and after exchanging a look with Torin, Cosra joins the retinue.

I admit that I expected something magical and grandiose when we reach the spring. Instead, we find a bubbling fount spilling from the rocky ground. The pile of rocks that stand out from the bit of wilderness. Some of the rocks are old and covered with moss. Others seem newer.

"It's tradition to add a pebble," Kei remarks with a shuttered face. Does he regret his moment of candor?

"This is it?" I ask no one in particular. I touch a few stones that are darker than others, not sure if I expect something to happen. But they are ordinary rocks and nothing of this shrine speaks to me. "Was she so easily forgotten?" I ask myself quietly. "Our books say that the First and Second Daughters were absorbed to protect the land."

Kol places a smooth white stone on top. "Our books have never said much. The First Daughter, after her sacrifice, disappeared. There was some talk that the Second Daughter was buried, but the location was hidden so that no one would desecrate her body. I confess I've never thought about how the tale differs in different kingdoms."

"I've always wondered," Kei says without any rancor towards his younger brother, "why the Third Daughter never returned. I mean, the stories say that she was thrown or cast or sent to the North. They never say she died. But if her sisters were dead, and she was truly envious, why didn't she come back?"

Kol's lips tilt up, and his dimples appear. "I've wondered the same."

The two brothers stand side by side with no animosity between them as I continue to explore the stacked stones. I brush aside some of the moss and freeze.

Cosra notices right away. "What is it?"

Neither Kol nor Kei notice her slip in formalities as my fingers trace a crescent-shape etching on one the stones. Were there more? I begin to clear some of the foliage as much as possible. Seeing my action, Cosra joins me. We uncover two more darker stones with the same crescent shape. There might be more, but the presence of three seems more than coincidence.

"I've never noticed that before," Kei says, his brow knitted in consternation, "but to be honest, I have only been here twice before."

"Father took me here once," Kol remarks, "and I remembered the spring. I didn't pay much attention to the rocks.".

A faint hum fills my ears. The medallion – the one Kel draped around my neck the day I was crown his queen – feels heavy against my chest.

I recall my dream last night, but I'm reluctant to mention

it. "I've seen this before," I say quietly. My now dirty fingers touch the three stones. The marked stones are interspersed among the regular stones: one is near the base of the pile, two are closer to the top where recent additions have been made.

"In a book?" Kol asks as he crouches near me and Cosra. "Your hands are dirty." He pulls out a kerchief from his pocket, but I indicate that I'll wash the dirt from my hands in the spring.

The moment my hand touches the icy spring water, heat radiates from the medallion on my chest, and I experience a vision far too similar to my dream, only this time the images are clear. Once more, I see the ageless woman on the ground in tears, dark hair veiling her face. The hooded figure holding the knife is ready to strike. But now I see a third person – another woman with dark hair – running towards them. The one on the ground looks up, and I see her face. Their faces... The crescent knife strikes several times. The hooded figure's slender hand swings the crescent-shaped knife relentlessly. The third woman screams and from her hands a bright light streams forth. The hooded figure with its feminine mouth tries to ward off the attack. Both streams of power collide, and the world explodes as I'm thrown out of the vision.

I cry out as Kol grabs me and shakes me to my senses. His face is pale, his eyes wide with worry. "Ilyria!" When I blink at him a few times, his hands clasp my wet fingers. "Your hands are freezing." He presses the kerchief around my fingers.

Cosra puts a hand to my cheek. "You weren't responding," she says worriedly. "It was like your mind was somewhere else."

Kei, his mouth pressed in a thin line, watches Kol rub my numb hands. "Are you alright?" he asks, but there is anger in his eyes as Kol continues to touch me.

My mouth opens and closes foolishly. I take a steadying breath. "I saw something," I whisper. Kol stills, his hands tightening as he takes in what I've said. "But I-I don't think I can talk about it yet." I'm on the verge of tears. The humming is gone, but I'm afraid to touch the medallion.

My three companions stare at me like I've lost my mind,

and maybe I have. I can't make sense of what happened. Was I hallucinating? I've always valued my mental capabilities. I could reason and argue with the best teachers in Fernwald. As a child, I confess I never placed much belief in the stories surrounding the First, Second, and Third Daughters. But this – whatever I saw – defies logic.

Cosra acts quickly to gain my attention. "Well, you can't stay kneeling like that forever." Her words are purposefully sharp to bring me to my senses, but both Kei and Kol glare at her bluntness.

"We need to head back," Kol murmurs in a gentler tone. He gets to his feet. "This was meant to be a brief respite. Can you stand?" Strong fingers beckon invitingly.

I take Kol's hand, grateful because my knees wobble alarmingly. When I falter, Kol holds me by the elbow with warm hands, and our eyes meet.

"I'll take the queen back," Cosra says taking my arm firmly from Kol.

It's only then that I notice Kei standing rigid, his face filled with something akin to jealousy. The older prince turns on his heel and stomps away. Startled, Kol begins to chase his brother, but when I move to follow, Cosra stops me and shakes her head.

"Let them be," she advises. "No man has a claim to you, remember that. Let them deal with their actions."

"But—"

"No buts. Power is an attractive thing, and you wield it naturally. Whichever prince you choose to be king must understand and value that. He must respect what and who you are."

I find myself asking, "What am I?"

Cosra drops her chin for a moment as we walk back to our horses. "Someone who can bring change."

XXIII: A GAME OF WILLS

Our scout informs us that the Northern force is on the move – and heading towards Pollux as we anticipated. This possibility was my motivation for moving sooner rather than later, and our advance has paid off. We hold at a ridge which gives us the vantage of the road and wait.

When they appear on the horizon, I'm surprised. From earlier reports, I expected a hodgepodge group of bandits or mercenaries. Instead, we see what appears to be an organized military force.

Even Kei is surprised. He wheels his horse around to talk to me. "My queen, you can't be at the front."

I don't bother to hide my flash of irritation. Do they honestly think I intend to lead a charge? "Is their force greater than ours?" What if I've miscalculated?

Kol maneuvers closer at my question. "No. But we'll take losses regardless." His grim expression tightens his jawline. It's not fair for him to be so attractive when he's this serious.

We don't know the Northern forces' skill. We are more heavily armored, but that means they'll be faster on their horses. I know enough about gear to know the advantages and disadvantages. But what is the purpose of their incursion? The force is not nearly big enough for an actual invasion.

As the two armies face each other and wait, a lone rider from the other side emerges waving a parley flag. The black cloth snaps in the wind. I signal to Torin to agree to a parley.

"Kei, Kol, and Torin, ride with me," I say as a group from the other side breaks off.

No one has time to argue with me because I move my horse forward. Torin signals for the archers to guard our move and hastens to my side. The two princes curse at what they perceive is impetuous behavior. I do my best to hide my smile.

As we near the meeting point, I analyze the four riders approaching us. They all wear helmets that are a mix of metal and leather, much like their armor, but I note that one of the riders has a wide red sash running across the chest.

Once we are at a civil distance from each other, the helmets come off. I hope my face betrays none of my surprise when I see that two of the riders are female. The woman with the red sash has streaks of gray in her dark hair. The other woman is younger, and her light brown hair is twisted into a braid.

"I am Aylin," she says with a nod at me. "Lord Bender's daughter." Her shrewd eyes scan me from head to toe.

"I am Ilyria of Tyre," I say somewhat impatiently. She may be older than me, but I refuse to be intimidated. Truth be told, I am intimidated, but I'm great at bluffing. "Why has the North invaded our lands?"

She scoffs at my words. "Invaded? I am simply taking what is rightfully ours."

I pretend to consider her words, glancing at my companions. Move and countermove. "So, this annual foray is to take back what is yours? And then you, pray tell, go back home and tell stories about it?"

Aylin smiles. "I see the child queen is wiser than she appears. Your predecessor was less bold and far less clever."

A quick warning glance at Kol to settle down. "Return home before winter closes the passage with snow," I advise. My hands clench my horse's reins, but I hope she doesn't see. "Your actions here are an act of war, and we will not hesitate to defend our people and our land." I wish I were taller so I would cut an imposing figure on a horse.

Aylin's eyes are an unusual shade of brown, and in the light, there is a reddish glint in them. "Tell me, child, what do you know of war? Have you fought against barbarians? Bears? Things that move only in the night?"

The younger woman next to her laughs mockingly. "She is barely out of the nursery."

I flush. Still, I won't be easily baited. I hear my brother's voice cautioning me. *Be calm. The first to lose his temper is the loser in any argument.* "We hold the field, and our forces are larger. There is no reason for anyone to lose their lives."

"I don't retreat, child," Aylin says condescendingly.

"Address her properly," Kol growls, his hand on the pommel of his sword. "She is the Queen of Tyre."

Aylin narrows her eyes on Kol, her lip curling in disdain before realization crosses her face. "You. I know of you. You are Alia's son."

At the mention of his mother, Kol blanches. "How do you —"

"If you live to see the morning, maybe I'll tell you," Aylin replies. "We won't retreat, and despite your *slightly* larger numbers, my men know how to deal with that. Istur remains ours."

I wheel my horse around and make a beeline to our army, Torin guarding my rear as Kol and Kei flank me. "Get the men ready," I order as we reach the relative safety of our side. I gesture to Cosra to bring my bow.

"What are you doing?" Kol asks. His brother stops to stare at me.

I don't answer them as I move up and down the line of men, meeting their eyes with mine. On impulse, I touch the medallion hidden beneath my shirt. I've been afraid to touch it since the shrine, but now it is a reassuring reminder of why I'm queen.

"I was not born in Tyre," I say as loudly as possible. "But King Kel chose me to be your queen, to guide and protect this land to the best of my ability. We must protect those that cannot fight for themselves, and we must defend our land. We will not go quietly; we will not shirk from our oath to defend our land."

I turn to face the potential battlefield. Kol, Kei, and Torin fan out from me, ready to direct the men into battle. And now the contest of wills: which side moves first?

The two sides clash, the heavy shields of Tyre facing the poles and spears of the North. From where I watch, the sound embeds itself in my memory. I see the red and black colors of Kol's men, and the orange and gold colors of Kei's. Torin is under orders to not split the men, so the army moves forward as a unified force.

I notch an arrow and aim high. The arrow flies true in the sky, curving upwards and above the din of the battle before landing away from the fighting. Kei sees the arrow and looks at me briefly in confusion. With his protective guard around him, he is not hard-pressed for defense. He probably thinks I've gone mad.

Then, on the horizon, comes an army carrying the green and gold colors of Fernwald. I wasn't sure until the other day that the force would come on time – Ronan must've had a stroke of luck to assemble them so quickly.

The Northern forces see their predicament too late. They are now cornered by us on one side and squeezed by Fernwald's military by the other. Although smaller in force, the Fernwald army is heavily armored and formidable. Escape is no longer possible.

I move forward, a group of assigned men leading the way to protect me. Torin notes my action and shouts corresponding orders. The men do not press their advantage and use shields to force the Northern forces into a taut circle.

Kol and Kei push their way towards me. Sweaty with a red mark on his cheek, Kol reaches me first. "What is this?" he demands, pushing his helm back.

"Our assurance of victory," I say as Torin parts the men to allow me to move into view.

In front of me, Aylin is furious and pale, but she holds her chin high when she sees me. Her soldiers mill around her, nervous and uncertain.

"Well played," she says to me, ripping off her helmet. She tosses it to the ground. "I did not see that coming."

"I have no wish for further bloodshed," I state. Kei and Kol move to my left and right respectively, but I keep my eyes on Aylin. "Your incursion into Tyre is over!"

"So, it appears." Aylin's horse prances a bit and tosses its head. The woman looks at the flags of Fernwald before she speaks again. "And what will you do now, little queen?" Her tone is deliberately mocking.

"Drop your weapons!" Torin orders. "The Queen offers mercy if you surrender!"

"They invaded Tyre!" Kei protests much to my astonishment. "They should be shown no mercy!"

The woman next to Aylin gawks at Kei, but I hold a gloved hand up for silence. "We are not butchers," I say in a quieter tone to Kei. When he opens his mouth to speak, Torin reaches over to grab the prince's reins. Kei's mouth snaps shut. With deliberate slowness, I notch an arrow and aim straight at Aylin.

"What are you doing?" Aylin asks, the first sign of panic in her face.

"You have twenty seconds to drop your weapons." I pause for dramatic purposes. "Anyone who refuses will be executed."

"You can't do that!" the woman next to Aylin shouts. "You can't kill us like we're criminals!"

"You have invaded our lands without provocation. I can and will execute you like common criminals. What say you? Be quick! My arm is getting tired."

"You're bluffing!" the woman screams, but Aylin gestures at her to be silent.

With resentful composure, Aylin drops her sword. Within seconds, more weapons are heard falling to the ground. Torin takes the lead to gather weapons and corral the weaponless Northerners. From the rear, Fernwald's forces let out a cheer.

A captain wearing a green and gold sash approaches me as I lower my bow. "Your Majesty, your brother sends his greetings and love," he says to me. "I have been instructed to obey you until we are dismissed. What are your orders?"

"How far to Istur?" I ask Kol.

"Less than an hour," the prince replies with a bemused

expression.

"To Istur. We camp there tonight."

XXIV: A MEETING OF MINDS

All I want is a bath (not to be had, unfortunately) and a bed. However, Cosra insists on cleaning one of the homes for my use before I can sleep. I'm too tired to argue. Kei and Torin and the captain from Fernwald secure the Northern prisoners, and I wander the town aimlessly. Kol refuses to leave my side.

"When?" he asks. "When did you contact your brother for help?"

If what you say is true, I need to find a way to corner the Northerners. After talking to Torin, my thought is to prevent them from retreating. Can you muster a sizeable force to enter Tyre from the east...?

My letter to Ronan and my desperate plea for help. I wasn't sure if the help would arrive in time. "I wrote to him before we left," I say with a mental note to write to Ronan and soon. "Do you know if we had significant casualties?"

Kol's dark brown eyes regard me seriously. "You timed everything." He lets out a heavy breath. "A handful of deaths on both sides. We were not in battle long enough to incur heavy losses. Your plan saved lives. Why didn't you tell me? Us, I mean."

"Because I wasn't sure." *And I wasn't sure you could be trusted.*

A hint of pain. "You still don't trust me or my intentions."

I don't get a chance to respond because Torin appears, and from his posture it is clear he's looking for me. I hail him.

"Lady Aylin," Torin says with a hint of sarcasm, "wants to speak to you."

Exhausted as I am, I could say no. But when my hand flutters to the medallion against my chest, I'm convinced that I need to see this woman and hear what she has to say.

Kol frowns. "You're not seeing her alone." When I raise a brow, he flushes. "Allow me to accompany you, at least."

Torin leads us to a building that he has turned into a makeshift jail. "We split them up to make them easier to handle, but no one seems interested in picking a fight right now. Still, we can't be too careful. Aylin and her second are the only women, so I've housed them here."

When we enter, I see the building is more like a simple home with a large open area that functions as a common area, a kitchen, and a study. A narrow staircase leads to a loft where there are beds.

Aylin has her hands loosely tied in front of her, an ineffective way of restraining her if anyone asks me. At my askance glance, Torin explains, "We've checked her for weapons, and her men are guarded well. They've been checked for weapons by Cosra, and the ties are meant to slow her down and hamper them should they try to escape."

Aylin snorts, and the woman next to her sneers at us. "We could have fought and killed many of you, but we didn't," the woman snaps.

"That's enough, Fay," Aylin cautions. "I want to speak to your queen alone."

"No." Kol's voice is hard, belligerent. "We have guards around, and Torin and I aren't leaving."

"What I have to say should not be heard by everyone," Aylin retorts, her mouth pressed into a thin line.

I cross my arms across my chest. "Torin, send the guards out. But you and Kol stay." When Aylin is about to protest, I interrupt her. "That is as much privacy as I'm allowing." No matter how skilled of a fighter, I have no doubt that Torin and Kol can protect me. I take a closer look at the woman named Fay. She's shorter, her face harder and with a cunning edge. Her hair is twisted into a messy knot on top of her head, and tangled strands dangle down her broad face. Like Aylin, her hands are tied loosely in front, but Torin's taken the extra precaution of doing the same to her feet.

Aylin waits until the guards leave the room before regarding me curiously. "Do you treat all your prisoners so well?" In her rustic leathers, she appears formidable even without weapons.

"I don't consider you a prisoner, but we would be mincing words to discuss it further," I say with a shrug. "What do you have to say to me?" I pause when I see the way her attention shifts to Kol. "Or is this about Kol?"

Kol's nostrils flare. "You knew my mother." A statement, but Aylin nods. "How did you know her?"

Aylin smirks. "She was my cousin," Aylin announces and lets out a huff when I stifle a gasp. "Our mothers were sisters. Do you know your heritage on your mother's side, Prince Kol?"

Based on her behavior, this woman is accustomed to command. Her speech is cultured and indicates that she's educated, so she's likely a noblewoman from the North. That's when I notice Kol's pale face. He suspects something, but what?

"What do you mean?" Kol whispers.

"Your birthright, Prince Kol. You don't just have Royal blood from your father's side. You have it from your mother's side as well." Aylin takes two dignified steps towards Kol. "Your great-uncle was King of the North."

Torin shifts, his hand resting on the pommel of his sword, but I stop him from acting. "Are you suggesting Kol is an heir to the throne?" I ask.

But Aylin ignores my question. Her eyes remain on Kol's ashen face. "The king had a younger brother who married my aunt, my mother's sister. They had a child. A daughter. Alia."

We take a moment to absorb that information, and for once I am glad that no one else is present. Fay watches us like a hawk – or a vulture.

"Th-that's not possible," Kol murmurs, shaking his head. He is pale and shocked.

When Kol becomes confused, Torin steps forward. "Why would anyone of that rank be traipsing about?" Torin barks.

Fay curls her lip. "Wouldn't you like to know?"

When Aylin shushes Fay, I find the action curious. Ronan would advise me to think why Aylin is revealing this now. "Say we believe you," I speak carefully, "and Kol is a relative of yours. Are you simply here for a reunion?" But then I start connecting the dots and curse my slow brain. Kol is of royal blood on both sides, and he may be the next King of Tyre. If Aylin speaks the truth, then Kol may have a claim to the throne in the North.

Alanna's cramped letter springs to mind. She was afraid and didn't trust either Kei or Kol. Why? When I look at Kol again, I wonder if he is truly shocked. What if that isn't shock on his face but fear? Had Kel and Alanna married, had she given him a child, Kol's position would be further from the throne. How convenient that Alanna died, Tassia died, and Kel died. How convenient for the North. How convenient for... Kol.

Something like physical pain lances through me as I stare at Kol. What if... *Why? Why does suspicion always fall on you, Kol? Why do I want to trust you?*

Kol, aware of my scrutiny, faces me with hurt eyes. He isn't a fool. "My queen," he whispers through bloodless lips. "No. No."

Fay's mocking laugh jars me to my senses. "It seems as though you're connecting the dots," Fay says.

Aylin, frowning, spins around in surprise. "Fay, that isn't —"

A commotion outside distracts us all, and suddenly, Kei storms into the room. "Why was I not notified that you were interrogating the prisoners?" he demands, grabbing me by the shoulders. "Why are you here alone with them? Don't you care about your safety?"

I push him back. I want to stomp my foot like a child. "I am not interrogating them," I hiss. We sound like we're squabbling children. "Your brother entrusted Tyre to me." I pull out the medallion. "Remember this, Kei? Remember that I was given this when I was crowned?"

Aylin makes a sound. "We're not here because of Prince Kol," she blurts. "We're here because of the Second Daughter!

Because of that!" And she points to the chain around my neck.

XXV: IN THE MIDDLE OF THE NIGHT

"What did you say?" I ask at the same time as Kol.

Aylin tosses her head. "Around my neck, I have a necklace like that." She lifts her chin so we can see the chain.

With a resigned sigh, Torin approaches her and with his thumb and forefinger, gingerly lifts the chain until a large onyx stone is revealed. It's similar to the stone in my medallion, but hers is etched with a crescent – the same shape we found at the shrine.

I take a step towards Aylin, but Kei grabs me and holds me close. Could he be a little less over-protective? But before I snap at him, I think about Kol and his potential blood tie to the North. Kei doesn't know anything about Kol's mother – and it should stay that way for now. When Kol looks over at me, I give a minute shake of my head. I only hope Aylin doesn't bring the topic up again. We should end this conversation soon.

"This black mineral is found only in the North," Aylin says quickly as if trying to convince me of something.

I gesture to the etching on the stone. "That mark – what is it?"

Fay sneers at us. "The Second Daughter's symbol. Don't you southerners know anything?"

"We've never had symbols associated with the Three Daughters," I retort. I'm beginning to dislike her. "It's not in our books. How did a black jewel from the North make it to Tyre?"

"Pry the stone out," Aylin says, and I gape at her. "Do it!"

"This is ridiculous," Kei snaps. "Ilyria, you need to rest. You can deal with this later."

Torin's mouth turns down at Kei's overly familiar tone, but he seems to agree with the prince. "Your Majesty," he says pointedly, "perhaps *Prince* Kei is right."

"Prince Kei," Fay echoes, and her broad face scrunches up.

Aylin continues to talk. "It's tradition for women to undertake a task when they come of age. Alia's was to place a stone at the Second Daughter's shrine because she is important to our history."

When Kei reacts to Kol's mother's name, I become anxious to end this. "Perhaps you are right, Kei. I am tired." Aylin opens her mouth to protest, but I quickly add, "We will discuss this later. Kei, Kol, come with me. Torin, ensure they are secure and comfortable." Torin knows me well enough to see through my orders.

Without further ado, I grab Kei's arm and drag him out of there. Kei sputters, but rather than look like a fool, adjusts his stride so we're walking side by side. Kol positions himself to my left.

"Why were those barbarians talking about Kol's mother?" Kei demands, glancing at his younger brother with a frown.

"It came up when we talked about the last time Tyre sent forth a force." Kol's lie is smoothly delivered.

An awkward silence falls between us, and I wonder if Kei believes Kol. When we reach the main home that Cosra's commandeered for me, I let all the exhaustion show. "Gentlemen, let's regroup in the morning. It's been a horribly long day."

"Ilyria," Kei says then stops. His lower jaw moves as he reconsiders his words. "Just don't wander around without letting me know." When I raise a brow, he adds, "Please."

Kol's nostrils flare. "I was with her. She is safe with me." The two brothers glare at each other.

What is up with these two? "Can we not?" I murmur. I shoo them away. "Just go." The guards at the front door move aside to let me through, and I don't look back as I enter the home.

Inside, Cosra has been industrious to say the least. The

home is simple and rustic, consisting of a huge room with stairs that lead to a curtained loft. Towards the right is a cheery hearth where Cosra has stirred up a fire to ward off the cold. A half-wall cordons off the kitchen. To the left is a sitting area of sorts and a scarred wooden table worn with years of use.

"I put fresh sheets on the beds up there," Cosra tells me as she pushes a pot filled with water closer to the fire. "The water should be plenty warm for you to wipe down. It won't be the luxury of the castle, but at least you won't stink so much."

I bite back a smile. "Thank you, Cosra. A solid floor to sleep on will do."

The woman sniffs, but her lips twitch. "You're an odd queen, that's for sure. And I heard those two men arguing over you." She hands me a cup of tea. "I checked it myself. You'll leave some coins for the owners of this home, mind you, since I raided their supplies."

I take the tea gratefully and eat the simple porridge Cosra's prepared. It's hot and filling. That's all that matters. "You don't really think Kol and Kei were fighting over me, do you?" I ask in hushed tones. Cosra's mouth twitches again. "Wait, you think that…" I trail off, unable to finish my words. My face feels like it's burning.

"Why do you doubt it so much?"

I stare into the fire. "Father used to say that I got the intelligence, but Alanna got all the beauty."

"Your father sounds like a dimwit," Cosra remarks. "So, that's what this is about." The woman folds her arms on the table. "You are not a true beauty like your sister, I won't lie. But you're not ugly either. You can be charismatic without being beautiful. And you have that, and you have a certain charm." She considers me with a critical eye. "Your best feature are your eyes. They are intelligent and clever. I have seen those two look at you when you talk. They admire you plenty, Ilyria, and I think it is because you are not a twit that those men find you fascinating."

"You don't think it's because of the throne?" I hate the uncertainty in my voice.

Cosra hums and cocks her head. "Perhaps a little. I don't know those two well enough to be sure." She refills my cup and waves off my thanks. "Power can be a lure, so yes, it is possible. But don't sell yourself short. Even King Kel, at the end, saw your value. Otherwise, you wouldn't be here as you are."

With the blessedly warm water, it's a refreshing but quick wipe down before I crawl into the bed. The sheets are rough, but I don't care. I fall asleep the moment my head hits the pillow.

XXVI: CONFESSION

I'm woken suddenly by Cosra shaking me. "Ilyria," she whispers anxiously. "Prince Kei is doing something odd."

When I sit up, Cosra explains that she was looking out the window and saw Kei sneaking around. He went to the building where Aylin is and made the guards inside leave.

I slept dressed in clean clothes, so I grab a cloak and head out, stopping briefly to ask one of the guards to get Torin to meet me there. Cosra and I make our way to the building, but when I see the guards outside looking confused, I gesture to them to remain silent before going to the side of the building where the window is slightly ajar.

"What did you tell them?" I hear Kei demand.

The annoying laugh is from Fay. "Nothing," the woman says. "But your brother now knows his mother was no commoner."

Kei curses.

"Fay, what are you talking about? You speak as though you know him," Aylin says in a ringing voice.

"In a way I do," Fay responds. "Aylin, if the old king had known that Alia had a son, would he have left the throne to his daughter? How do you think our queen truly feels about Alia's only child?"

"Queen Enre has three sons," Aylin says, shocked. "Why would she worry?"

"Because Kol was born before the sons, and before the old king died," Kei replies.

So, Kei knows about Kol's lineage. But how? And when? I

grab Cosra's arm anxiously.

"That's why the prince is here," Fay says. "Because we have a common goal."

"Fay, what have you done?" Aylin asks in horror. "Have you been working with this man?"

"Indirectly," Kei says.

Fay laughs again. "Enre wants the threat to her crown gone. And Kei wants the throne of Tyre."

"Shut your mouth, woman," Kei snarls. "You are not to talk about this with Queen Ilyria."

"Oh, ho, ho. Are you worried I might tell her something? You could be just rid of her!"

Kei snarls, "You will not touch her!"

"That sounds like our agreement is coming to an end," Fay says with mock sadness. "We did try to end her."

"I told you to stop," Kei snaps, and I hear him pacing. "I told you not to harm her!"

"We got rid of her sister for you," Fay sneers, "and gave Tassia the means to poison Ilyria. You were supposed to let Tassia kill Ilyria and then accuse Tassia. Two birds, one stone."

My eyes close in pain. Not Kol at all. Kei. Kei caused my sister's death.

Heavy breathing. "You will not touch Ilyria. Ever." A deadly tone fills Kei's voice. "Both of you."

"I have no interest in harming the Queen of Tyre," Aylin says, desperate and worried.

"It doesn't matter." A sword is drawn.

Someone gasps. "You will strike down defenseless women?" Aylin cries.

There is a commotion and a scream. Cosra and I run to the front as the guards burst through the doors. I push my way forward and stop.

Aylin is on the ground, a wicked slash to her arm.

Kei has his sword embedded in Fay's stomach, the woman glaring at him with hatred in her eyes. But his eyes are pinned on the hair pin in his shoulder. Blood dribbles from Fay's lips as she smiles, but the light is already fading from her eyes.

Kei's hold on his sword loosens, and Fay drops to the ground. Kei's hand grabs the hair pin, and he stumbles back.

"The pin," Aylin gasps. "It's poisoned."

Kei sees me, Cosra, the guards as color fades form his face. He drops to his knees.

I don't think. I react and run to him, kneeling to reach him.

"Ilyria." My name escapes his lips in confusion. "Sorry." His body sways and falls against me.

"Kei!" I cry out, holding him with both hands.

Kol, frozen in horror, finally moves. With Kol's help, I lie Kei down, supporting his head on my lap.

"Clear the room!" Torin roars at the guards as Cosra tends to Aylin. His somber face takes in the scene again. "Cosra, get the physician for the prince."

Aylin grabs Cosra's arm. "The poison. It's fatal. There is no cure." She winces as Cosra applies a compress to her would. "Ilyria, I'm sorry. But when Kei attacked, Fay pulled the pin and stabbed him. There isn't anything we can do."

We absorb that information, and I'm too stunned to do anything but weep. I want to say it isn't true, but when I touch Kei's skin – cold and clammy – I know it's true. He's dying.

Torin helps Aylin stand. "We will take her to the physician," he says in a low voice.

When Cosra and Torin leave with Aylin, I'm left with Kei and Kol.

"Sorry," Kei whispers again. "It was me, Ilyria. Your sister died because of me." His beautiful eyes close. "I thought... Kel would choose me." He coughs.

Aylin had told us the poison was fatal and had no cure, but I still couldn't accept that Kei would die. "Why?"

Kei grimaces as a spasm of pain wracks his body. "I wanted to be king," he wheezes between spasms. He blinks and looks at me. "You were... The ambush. You were to die then. But you—you changed everything." A tear escapes an eye as he searches my face for something. "Tassia. Before I knew you. Tassia. I told her to get rid of you."

Kol sits back on his haunches. "Did you kill Tassia to silence her?"

Kei nods and brings my hand to his lips. "I changed. You ch-changed me."

Tears fall from my eyes, but I'm barely aware of them. It all makes sense now. Kei continues to whisper his confession. He explains how the goal was to get rid of Alanna and Tassia and make the lords suspect Kol was behind everything. He hadn't expected Kel to arrange a marriage by proxy, so he included himself to bring me to Tyre.

"Every time I saw you... I couldn't do it. I couldn't hurt you." The spasms are less frequent as his breathing becomes labored. "I could woo you. Be king... that way. But... I couldn't. You... so pure. Wonderful. Don't... hate me."

I don't know what to do or say. I push sweat-dampened hair from his face. "I don't hate you. Kei, I forgive you. For everything." I choke back a sob.

A faint smile. "I never... deserved you. I..."

"It's okay," I say as gently as possible. "You can rest now."

Kei turns his head towards Kol. "Brother. Kol. My baby... brother."

Kol doesn't bother to hide his tears. "I forgive you," he says. "Please, don't die." He words end on a choked sob.

But Kei shakes his head, squeezing his eyes shut. "Be brave, Kol." When he opens his eyes, he looks at me. "I'm scared. Don't... leave me."

I stroke his hair back. I should be angry. I should hate him. He is responsible for Alanna's death. But as the poison continues to work its way through his body, I can't bring myself to feel anything other than intense sorry. "I'm here. We're both here."

A shaky breath escapes his bloodless lips. "I... love... you. I wanted... to... be..." His eyes close briefly, and when they open, they are pain-free and bright. He gazes at me. "Your eyes... stars. I... love..." A wheeze.

"Rest," I murmur. "Be at peace, Kei."

Kei lets out a small sound. His eyes grow unfocused as his rattled breath ends and his chest stills. His hold on my hand loosens.

Alanna. Kel. Now Kei. All this time, I've held back my tears, my sorrow, my internal fear, and terror. I'm not yet twenty, and I am old with grief. I think back to the girl I used to be. Lonely but free. Knowledgeable but ignorant. Wise but naïve. And then I think of what I am now: a person surrounded by death. It's too much. I weep for Alanna, for Kel, for Kei, and for the girl I once was.

XXVII: ECHOES

I cry until I become a shell with a name but nothing of substance within. Cosra tends to me. Torin fusses. Someone carries me to a bed and tucks me in. As bad as it sounds, I need to be selfish, and that means I don't have the capacity to console Kol. Besieged by death, the world has lost rhyme and reason.

There are questions I have, but for now they are meaningless. Kei. He brought about Alanna's death. He's the reason we were ambushed on my way to Tyre. I should hate him. Why can't I? Towards the end, he wanted to repent. We were not friends, but I was not his enemy. I understand now his words and his warning to me. He knew that no matter what, if the truth were known, he would be found unworthy.

Love. Kei said he loved me, and I don't know how to process that information. Love. Growing up in Alanna's shadow, I made so many assumptions about what my life would be like. As I examine his actions, I think there must be some truth to his words. Affection, at the very least. Perhaps there was something more. Oddly enough, that acknowledgment causes a kind of pain I'm unfamiliar with.

After I've shed all my tears, after I fall asleep exhausted, I wake to find Cosra's worried face hovering within my line of vision. My body aches: this is what it's like to feel emotionally battered. But I am grateful for Cosra's warm presence. I miss Cymoni. "Cosra, ask Torin to bring Aylin to me," I request in a hoarse voice. I need to stay busy.

Cosra opens her mouth to protest, but perhaps she senses that I need to occupy my mind because she nods and dips her head with unusual gravity. I let her fuss over me. By the time Aylin arrives, I'm vaguely presentable, bundled by the fire because I feel chilled to the bone.

Torin lingers and looms over Aylin – he won't leave me unguarded especially in my state. But Aylin isn't a threat. The proud woman is a shadow of herself, and I wonder if Fay's actions (and her links to Queen Enre) have shaken her as much as Kei's confession has shaken me. With her hair in disarray, her wounded arm tended to by our physician, her cocky assurance is gone, and in its place is a very human bewilderment.

Facing the fire, I wait until she sits with Torin near her. "Will your queen come for Kol?" I ask, my voice sharper than I intended. I don't have time to beat around the bush.

Aylin crosses her legs at the ankles under the guise of considering my words, but I suspect she's composing herself to respond honestly. "I don't know." Her dark eyes flicker with sadness. "Is he not the future King of Tyre? Will Tyre treat him better than his mother? Perhaps Enre will think that one throne is enough for Kol and leave him alone."

Her shock at Fay's actions was genuine, so what she says is pure speculation. Still, I have yet to uncover why she invaded my kingdom. "Are you familiar with your queen? Do you know her well?"

"We are kin by marriage, but she doesn't keep counsel with me," Aylin says. "I don't think she wants a war, but she is protective of her children."

"Then why send you? Why keep sending men yearly to Istur?" I demand, tapping the armrest with my fingers.

She gestures at the medallion around my neck that I wear in the open. "Have you looked at the stone?"

The medallion has been in the Tyre Royal Family for many generations. Do I dare damage it just to satisfy my curiosity? I remove it and stare at the shiny gem-like stone. When I begin to poke at the stone, Torin makes a sound in his throat. Wordlessly, I hand the medallion to him. He worries at the stone with a stiletto, and after a minute, a slight pop follow.

When the smooth stone is deposited in my hands, I see nothing odd. But then I flip it over to the flattened side and gasp. There, carved in crude form, is the crescent shape.

"The mark of the Second Daughter," Aylin says quietly. "In the North, she is a hero having protected people from her oldest sister. Before the Third Daughter died in the North, she claimed the lands would reunite under the Second Daughter again. Since then, all second daughters from the main houses in the North send stones to place at the Second Daughter's shrine. We come every year to mark that occasion and deliver the stones."

"Alia?"

"Had an older sister that died a few days after birth. Technically, Alia was the second daughter."

I try not to think about my similar connection. "But why not ask to make the journey? Why push innocents from their homes?" I quell the rising indignation with difficulty.

"I may be able to answer that," Torin says with a cough. "This predates some of your time, my queen, but we – Tyre and Fernwald – have always been hostile with the North, as you know. There is no trade between the lands, and when the North came down with less than a formidable host, Prince Kol's mother was forced into slavery."

"But if what Aylin says is true, then our prejudices are unfounded." Perhaps that comment was unnecessary, but I can't help but think aloud. I consider the possibility that my dreams have revealed a type of truth. "The truth may be something in between our history and that of the North's."

"We are still your prisoners, are we not?" Aylin asks rhetorically.

"You are." I bend my head. I sigh as I decide my next action. "We will escort you to the Northern Passage and release you." My voice hardens. "Unless you want a war, you will ask for permission to make the pilgrimage to the shrine. I will do my best to guarantee it. But you are not to send a military force into Tyre ever again. The next time it happens, I will consider it an act of war, and I will tell your queen as such."

The older woman tilts her head. "This would require correspondence between our lands."

"I expect it. No, I demand it," I amend my words to sound more assertive. I may never know the extent at which Enre meant to meddle in Tyre's affairs, but if Fay spoke the truth, Enre shares the blame for Alanna's death. It's difficult to push aside personal vendettas, but the people's lives are not something I plan to gamble with. If Enre will leave Tyre alone, I will open up a dialogue and find a peaceful solution. "You will carry a letter from me to your queen. Torin will take you back until we are ready to leave."

Aylin stands. "Perhaps someday, we'll understand why the Second Daughter's mark was hidden within a relic."

"Perhaps. Perhaps it was meant for this very moment," I reply.

Aylin bows before she leaves.

XXVIII: SHADOWS THAT CAME BEFORE

There is no way to provide a proper burial for Kei. His body would never survive the journey back home. The funeral pyre is built and lit. After the fire dies, we will gather what remains for entombment in the Royal Crypt.

Kol and I remain as solitary witnesses after the pyre is lit. Torin has his orders, and the men are busy preparing to return home. I have not spoken to Kol about his brother's death, but the death of two brothers in so short of a span must be hard to bear.

"What will you tell his mother?" Kol's soft inquiry startles me.

To be honest, I haven't given it much thought, but I realize now that I need an answer. During our short acquaintance, Lady Fleura has come across as both proud and broken. This will devastate her. "I will say he died protecting Tyre to his best ability. It isn't a lie. In the beginning, his motives were not pure. But I want to believe that in the end, he wanted to make it right. It benefits no one to reveal anything else."

The heat from the funeral pyre breaks the morning chill. No doubt I reek of smoke. We both do.

"That is beyond generous," Kol finally says with a catch in his voice.

"You loved him and Kel. I'm sorry." A glance tells me that Kol is lost in his thoughts.

"We both lost. A king. A brother. A sister. A husband. A friend. And I don't know—" He breaks off.

I state the inevitable truth, "You will be king soon."

The wind shifts the direction of the smoke and fans the flames brighter. But as the flames burn the wood and body and turn much of it into ashes, there is no closure for me or for Kol.

"And when I'm king, what will you do?" Kol asks.

"I'm not sure. Return to my brother, perhaps." Yet do I belong in Fernwald? I think about my time as Tyre's queen and wonder if I can return to anything less than that.

Kol looks at me. "You will leave Tyre?"

I don't answer, but as the funeral pyre is reduced to rubble, I tell him of my conversation with Aylin. He is silent as I talk about the Second Daughter and my concerns regarding Enre.

"I agree we should release them and send them back," he finally says, and I realize he speaks to me as my equal rather than as a subject or a king. "As for the North's queen..." He doesn't continue, but when I glance at him, he shakes his head. "There were times when I thought I should just give Kei the throne. He wanted it. He didn't have to—" He stops again, his throat moving with emotion. "All this time, I've never seen you cry until yesterday."

"I wondered if I was turning to stone," I say wearily. "I kept busy so I wouldn't need to think about it. There's been far too much loss, and no matter how many times I turn it over in my head, I wonder why. Why did Kei feel so desperate? Why did he act that way?"

"Sometimes there are no answers."

"Are you..." I hesitate. "Are you going to be alright?"

Kol checks to see that our conversation is private before answering. "Do we have a choice? Do I have a choice?"

I know what it's like to be trapped by life. This wasn't always the case. I had been the privileged younger sister, free to do as I please. When Alanna died, life changed so rapidly that I never got the chance to question anything. I had to adapt and bend with changes. But now... now I can reflect. The North remains a risk, but it is one where we have time. I am Queen for a little while longer, but the decision has been made for me. I won't need to choose. Perhaps Kol would have been my pick anyway. After so much turmoil, perhaps there might be time to rest and contemplate and properly grieve.

"You have choices, but they are of a narrow window," I breathe, the smoke stinging my eyes. "I think you love Tyre. You will be a good king."

He seems displeased or disappointed by my answer because he turns away. "I don't want to stand here anymore and watch a body burn." There is hurt and pain etched in the lines of his face. "It's just a body now. It isn't him." He starts to walk away. "You will always… have a place in Tyre."

XXIX: LEARNING TO WALK AGAIN

After we send Aylin back – there is now an unspoken understanding between her and me – Kol and I return home. The journey is quiet, less hectic, somber. I can't say whether I avoid Kol or Kol avoids me. Regardless, we barely speak except in passing, and perhaps we're afraid what we will say while we feel so raw.

When we arrive at the castle, anxious courtiers wait and observe. Perhaps some inkling of our grave news leaks because Lady Fleura is there. Kei's mother searches our party for Kei and is quick to note his absence. As I approach her, I realize she knows – I barely have to open my mouth before she cries. Her wails fill the courtyard as Kol stands with a box holding Kei's remains. It's a grim task, but Kol refused to let anyone else handle the box. And I do what I can to soften the blow: I lie and tell her Kei died protecting Tyre. The only ones who know of his betrayal are me, Kol, Torin, and Cosra. I hope it remains forever buried.

I want to sleep for a week, but I am only given a night's reprieve before I learn from Cymoni all that has transpired in my absence. As expected, the lords formed camps – one for Kol and one for Kei – and found ways to argue about the succession without my presence. Arguments and legal documents drafted are now pushed aside. There is only one obvious successor.

Kei becomes a martyr to his supporters and mother, and it does not bolster support for Kol with his Northern blood. That worries me. Kings have been overthrown for far less reasons.

"You are no longer the girl who left Fernwald," Cymoni

observes a week after our return. She sets the tea kettle close to the fire to keep warm. "It's the weight of the crown, and you've had your share of troubles."

I worry at a thumbnail. "I thought the lords would give up arguing – and they have," I say sourly. "But they are not united behind Kol."

Cymoni's old eyes narrow on me. "That will be his concern, not yours. Or is there more to this worry?"

When I don't respond, she takes me over to my dressing table and encourages me to sit. With gentle hands, she begins to brush my hair rhythmically and some of the tension leaves my shoulder.

"He's handsome," she finally says. "A stronger man than King Kel ever was."

"Cymoni!" Shocked, I tilt my head back to glare at her.

The old woman shrugs. "I am too old for niceties, child. You underestimate yourself. You always have. You only see value in this," she taps my head, "and in little else. Even before you became a widow, I saw the way the princes looked at you. You confused them, intrigued them, and challenged them. You made them think, and by doing so, they thought about you."

I make a face. "Ugh. I sound manipulative."

"No. But that is why they saw you as more than a queen." She smiles. "Your late husband wanted to keep you for Tyre. He knew you were good for the kingdom."

I shake my head. "I can't trap Kol into a marriage." Kol lamented his loss of choice. How could I take more of his life away by forcing him to marry me?

"How can a clever girl be so blind?" Cymoni sighs. "Have you ever allowed your heart to feel? Look at the prince not with logical eyes but with your heart. You hide behind that mind of yours because you're afraid. But when you're unguarded, you look at him as a woman not as a queen."

"No, I don't." The denial is swift, but it causes Cymoni to grin widely. My face grows hot. It's true that at times I admired Kol, but I also cautioned myself from admiring him too much because...

"You were afraid his interest was related to the throne," Cymoni says gently. "But now think of yourself. You deserve to love and be loved. We all do."

I duck my head. "What do I do?"

"Do what you always do, my dear. Seek out the truth. But this time, let your heart be the guide."

XXX: MOVING FORWARD

I learn from Torin that Kol is in the Royal Crypts. Torin stays with the guards so I can meet with Kol privately.

When I descend the steps, my slippered feet making little sound, the torches cast my shadow towards Kol. But he doesn't turn or acknowledge me when I reach his side. We stand before the two sarcophagi: a king and a bastard-born prince. Both brothers to Kol. He loved them both, regardless of their mothers and philosophical differences. His face, capable of warrior fierceness in one turn and open-minded wonder another, is lost in sorrow.

He is dressed in black velvet. Next to him, in the dim lighting, my dark blue gown could be black as well.

"Kol," I begin, "we need to—"

"No."

I'm surprised by the finality in his tone, and when I face him, he avoids my gaze, walking up to Kel's tomb to lay a hand on it. He bends his head, his mouth moving silently.

"I won't be king," he says finally. "I don't want to be king by default."

Reluctant to invade his personal space, I keep my distance. "At one point, you wanted to be king, didn't you?"

His slanted, dismissive look speaks volumes. "Is that what you think?"

"You may not be pleased under the circumstances by which it has become rightfully yours, but the throne is rightfully, lawfully yours, Kol." My hands are open in supplication. "Why would you refuse it?"

Kol's laugh is sharp and bitter. "Shall I confess before my

brothers? Before my mother?" He gestures to the alcove where his mother lies near my sister. "Before my father? Why not? What else do I have to lose?" The lines of his face are taut with emotion. "Do you remember when I said Kel didn't deserve you?" At my tiny nod, he grimaces. "I spoke too much of the truth then, but I don't regret my words. I meant them."

"What are you trying to say?"

He lets out a heavy breath. "I was bringing my brother's wife and queen to him, and we were attacked. I kept thinking I can't let her come to harm. She is my brother's wife. Brilliant, thoughtful, and kind. Qualities of a good queen. But she didn't flee. She came out of her carriage without fear or temerity. Brave. Clever. She refused to run and helped us fight. I could not stop thinking about her. I knew I should tell her about Tassia, but I thought that maybe if she began to hate me, it would be easier to feel less. I forgot that she was no ordinary woman. Instead, she reacted with dignity, and I lost her trust. Even then, she abolished slavery as her wedding gift. Of all the things she could have chosen... I didn't deserve her grace. Not only did Kel not deserve her, but I was no better. And what kind of brother has thoughts about his brother's wife?"

My mouth opens in shock, and Kol's eyes narrow at my reaction. "What you're saying can't be true," I whisper. "I am not any of those things."

"You judge yourself by a superficial standard." Kol's mouth flattens as his hand plucks at the peach fuzz on his neck. "You don't see how others see you, Ilyria. How I see you. Every day, I saw Kel leave you for Tassia, spending his time in leisure while you worked for the kingdom. Even Tassia recognized your value before Kel did. When Kel died, I couldn't help but wonder if somehow, by wishing that one day I could be worthy of you, I didn't invite Kel's death."

I shake my head. "You aren't to blame, Kol. You never were. You have a chance now to rule and set things right the way you see fit."

"You and I both know I don't deserve the throne. If you

proclaim me king, I will abdicate and return the throne to you."

Exasperated, I take a step towards him. "Why are you being like this? Kel never wanted me to rule long-term. You know that!"

"Because I want to earn the throne by merit, not by birthright or by pity or by being the only choice," he snaps, eyes wide and incredulous. "I want to be your choice, Ilyria."

I press a fist to my mouth and gather myself despite being confused by his behavior. With a sigh, my hand drops to my side. "Kol, you were always my first choice. My only hesitation was whether the lords would truly accept you."

Something I say makes Kol suck in his breath, hope flaring and dying in an instant. "Your first choice? For the throne and nothing else?" When my brow furrows, he says, "Let me phrase it this way. If I become king, what will you do?"

"I suppose it depends on how you transition from my rule to yours." I brush aside Kel's penned wish to have me remain in Tyre. "My brother would be more than happy to have me return home, so I needn't impose on your hospitality for long."

"And what if you're someone I want around? Here in Tyre? Would you stay?" His lips twist bitterly when I'm rendered speechless. "What's wrong with keeping you queen? I would serve you faithfully. No one can deny that you haven't done an incredible job so far. Stay here in Tyre. With m—with the people who have come to love you."

A strange feeling spreads in my chest, but I don't want to believe it. "Kol, what are you trying to say to me?" I find myself asking. Maybe I'm not as clever or intelligent as I think I am, but I know I need him to speak plainly.

"I can't live without purpose and passion," he begins with annoying obtuseness. "To me, the two must be intertwined. If you leave, I will have neither of those. Ilyria, I don't want the throne because I don't want you to leave. I won't ask you for anything other than the pleasure of serving you. I will be – content just to be near you."

All my books and studies have not prepared me for this. "Kol, are you saying you like me?" I have never felt so stupid in my life.

He rocks back on his heels. "I'm saying I'm in love with you," he nearly shouts at me. "I have been for some time."

"But I-I... Are you sure? I mean, men like you don't lo— fall for women like me," I stammer. Kol is handsome, beautiful, physically perfect.

"Women like you?" he echoes. "Ilyria, you're beautiful. To me, you're perfect. You are calm and wise when you need to be. You are brave against adversity. You stand for what you believe in. I could listen to you read aloud for hours. You *are* my purpose and passion."

Stunned speechless, I stand there awkwardly as the light in Kol's eyes dim in disappointment. Cymoni's advice reminds me that I need to pay attention to my heart more. I reach out with my hand to tuck an errant lock of hair behind his ear, my movement slow and wondering, and our eyes meet. Something kindles inside me. Kol stays still as my fingers trace the shape of his cheek, the angle of his jaw. I marvel how I can be so bold in this moment, and I want to explore what I'm feeling even further. "You need to become king," I say helplessly.

Kol swallows, his breathing uneven, when my fingers brush his lips, and I don't pull away when he peppers my fingers with light kisses. "You need to be queen," he whispers against my fingers. "If you want me to be king, then be my queen, my true queen. No concubines, no one else. A marriage of equals."

I whisper back, "Are you proposing to me?"

Kol drops to one knee while holding my hand to his face. "This isn't the way I wanted to win you, but if you will let me, I think you could be happy. I think I could make you happy."

"Purpose and passion," I murmur, repeating his earlier words.

"Will you... marry me, Ilyria?"

I stare at this man before me and answer with my heart. "Yes, Kol, I will."

XXXI: A NEW BEGINNING

The day after my reign as Queen ends, I marry Kol and my reign as Kol's queen begins. Oddly enough, our nuptials are met with approval by all the lords, and it gives me hope that Tyre can present a unified front.

Efforts to communicate with the North don't proceed as smoothly.

"If Queen Enre thinks I'm into empire building, she's sadly mistaken," Kol scowls. A few months into his reign and he scowls. "I have no interest in the North." He drums his fingers on the table.

"We have yet to hear from Aylin directly. That worries me," I confess. "We know nothing of Enre's character or motivations, and until we do, all thoughts are simply conjecture."

Kol regards me with heavy lidded eyes. "I love it when you talk like that." He moves to grab me, but I evade him and smack his hand gently. "Why are you being cruel?" he pouts.

"Cruel? I'm trying to keep you focused."

"I can focus with you on my lap."

I roll my eyes in mock dismay, but when he reaches for me again, I let him pull me to his lap. I admit that I was first smitten by him. Love blossomed gradually on my side, but it did blossom. I love him, and I've found new things to love about him. I love how his nose wrinkles when he laughs hard. I love the way he picks at the peach fuzz on his chin when he's thinking hard. I love the way he won't look at me when he's embarrassed. He's taught me to love and value myself.

"We now have a sizeable force in Istur," Kol says, playing with my unbound hair. "And now that we have the trade alliance with your brother, we shouldn't run into supply issues. So... we wait. It would be foolish of the North to try anything militarily. I'd like to use their devotion to the Second Daughter as a starting point for dialogue."

"I've been uncovering more about the Second Daughter in the vast library that no one visits," I say after a while. "It makes me wonder why we placed so much value on the First Daughter."

"It made for a better story?" he suggests. "Wait, are you thinking about the story Aylin told you? About the land being reunited under a Second Daughter?"

"I'm more curious about knowing the truth, but I doubt that will ever be feasible. At least I haven't had any more dreams about the Three Daughters."

"Whatever happened at the shrine was real," Kol states, "and as odd as it sounds, I do think somehow the spirit of the Second Daughter was trying to tell you the truth. But I don't want you visiting the shrine and dipping your hand in the water just to learn more."

"I very much doubt I'll be traveling in the near future," I murmur.

"We have a lot going on," Kol agrees.

"Mm-hmm. But also, Cymoni would never let me go."

Kol laughs, his nose scrunching slightly. "You should remind her that you are Queen and fully grown."

I give a secret smile and lower my eyes. "Yes. But she'll override me on this one. She won't want me gallivanting in my condition."

Kol stiffens. "Condition?" His brown eyes search my face. "Ilyria? Are you?" His hand rests on my stomach.

I nod and peek at him nervously. "Are you... happy?"

Kol embraces me fiercely. "I don't know if such a simple word can encompass what I'm feeling. A child. We're going to have a child." His kiss is tender. "Thank you."

"It did take two to produce this child," I tease.

"Thank you for staying with me," Kol amends, linking our hands together. "We'll be careful. You'll be careful. And we'll find a way to explore what happened with the Second Daughter. We'll do it together."

I kiss Kol on the lips. "Together."

ABOUT THE AUTHOR

Lj Byrne

LJ Byrne lives in the Twin Cities with her husband, two kids, two bunnies, and a very fluffy cat. An engineer by education, a scientist at heart, a writer in her soul, she's had an avid imagination since youth. She's a self-taught speed reader and full of useless facts and information, and her friends call her the female Cliff Claven. She likes strong female characters who don't back down - ever.

https://www.goodreads.com/author/show/20244678.L_J_Byrne

Twitter: www.twitter.com/LJByrne2
Instagram: www.instagram.com/authorljbyrne
Author Page: www.ljbyrnebooks.com

www.ingramcontent.com/pod-product-compliance
Lightning Source LLC
LaVergne TN
LVHW050313160826
845677LV00014B/3373

* 9 7 9 8 3 7 1 0 2 3 7 6 6 *